T0022665

Dead End Roads

S. Briney

authorHOUSE®

AuthorHouse™
1663 Liberty Drive
Bloomington, IN 47403
www.authorhouse.com
Phone: 1-800-839-8640

© *2010 S. Briney. All rights reserved.*

No part of this book may be reproduced, stored in a retrieval system, or transmitted by any means without the written permission of the author.

First published by AuthorHouse 11/20/2010

ISBN: 978-1-4520-8357-5 (sc)
ISBN: 978-1-4520-8358-2 (e)

Library of Congress Control Number: 2010915460

Printed in the United States of America

This book is printed on acid-free paper.

Because of the dynamic nature of the Internet, any Web addresses or links contained in this book may have changed since publication and may no longer be valid. The views expressed in this work are solely those of the author and do not necessarily reflect the views of the publisher, and the publisher hereby disclaims any responsibility for them.

Acknowledgments

I must thank the personnel of AuthorHouse for their professional assistance and guidance in the publication of this book.

My sincere appreciation also goes to a friend and a truly professional graphic artist, Gale Cochrane-Smith of Shadow Ridge Graphics, who can always provide the perfect photograph I need or an assist wherever it's needed. I also value her critique of my work. And to author Treva Tindol, I also express my thanks for her thoughtful comments regarding the psychological implications of this anthology.

And last, I thank my wife, Priscilla for tolerating my mood while writing this book and for her helpful criticism and technical computer assistance in editing each story.

Contents

From the Author····································ix

Fantasy Locked in a Criminal Mind····················1

The Rio Grande Connection·························16

Ridin' to the End of the Panhandle Rainbow··········23

Ultimate Retaliation·······························29

Barry Draper···································36

Identical Difference·······························42

Following the Weather Pattern·····················51

Chico··57

From the Author

Throughout our lives each of us must continually make choices as to which of two roads we choose to follow. These two roads lead in completely opposite directions as illustrated in the following stories.

One road leads to a happy, fulfilling and productive life. This is a life enriched with love, honor, and respect for one's Creator, country, family, and fellow man.

The opposite road often brings disrespect, jealousy, denial, unhappiness, violence, and often self-destruction. This road often becomes DEAD END.

The stories herein are strictly fictitious. Likewise are the characters and their names. Some locations and descriptions are based on fact, but I have taken liberties in their use to assist in creating both drama and impact when and where I deemed necessary.

As each story unfolds for the reader, it is my sincere hope that the personality of each of the characters will become real in every sense. By each story's end I want those characters to remain in their thoughts long after.

S. Briney

Fantasy Locked in a Criminal Mind

"Do you have any last words?" asked the warden.

"I'm sorry," was the mumbled faint whisper.

With those two words the warden removed his glasses giving the executioners the signal outside the chamber's mirror glassed window to begin the intravenous flow of the lethal liquids. The time was 6:03 P.M. in the Walls unit of the Texas Department of Justice prison in Huntsville, Texas. The slender white man strapped down face up on the gurney appeared much older than his years. He gave a deep final inspiration then a sigh and it was over.

At 6:10 P.M. the warden and prison chaplain left the chamber. Two officers entered and began the final preparations for the transfer of Jeremy Lee Kendall's body from the small room. The death certificate must yet be prepared for the record and the body will later be placed in the ground at the Huntsville prison cemetery. The entire ordeal had gone smoothly and with precision.

Jeremy Kendall's attorney who had commanded the initial defense at his murder trial and had spirited the numerous court appeals over the past six years slowly rose from his seat. Seated beside him in the chamber's adjoining room were two newspaper and television journalists. There were no family members present to witness the execution. The reporters followed the attorney out of the room in silence. Each felt a sick emptiness. Earlier this day a request to the Texas governor had failed to bring a reprieve.

1

Just outside the prison gates a handful of people both young and old had gathered and were huddled together trying to shield themselves from the damp biting Texas winter wind. Joining them was the usual cadre of reporters and television photographers that routinely gather in Huntsville whenever an execution is scheduled. On this night the usual few cardboard placards spelling protest of capitol punishment were displayed before the cameras. The events of the evening and the presence of this small protest group were certain to make the lead story later this evening on the 10 P.M. television news across the state. This activity has been common for each scheduled execution in Texas, yet Jeremy Kendall's date with death was somehow accentuated by his being responsible for a police officer's death as well as the death of another person.

The tragic events associated with Mr. Kendall's destructive walk through life were happenstance in part and not entirely by his own creation. As a matter of fact, the real story of Jeremy Kendall had actually begun years before his birth.

Young Billy Joe Sampson first met pretty Nell Ilene Crandall in Dodge City, Kansas one hot, humid summer afternoon in 1953. The twenty-one year old cowboy had received his professional rodeo card the year before for the PRCA (Professional Rodeo Cowboy Association). Slowly he had been gaining self- confidence and recognition as a professional saddle bronco rider at rodeos across the country.

Nell at nineteen was a very pretty tall slender young woman with beautiful long auburn hair. She came from a ranching background in Oklahoma. Since the age of fourteen she had been competing in the rodeo sport of barrel racing. She too had been making her mark as an outstanding performer in the sport.

Billy Sampson's love for rodeo had a much deeper meaning than just for the sport. For him, the rodeo competitors were not only friends but also "family". They represented a family which he had tragically lost as a young boy. His young Marine father had lost his life fighting the Japanese on the sands of Iwo Jima during World War II. Only six months later, his mother died in an auto accident near their home in west Texas. Her car was struck by a drunk driver. With his parents gone, young Billy was raised for a time by his elderly aunt.

While still attending high school, Billy began working as a hand on a nearby cattle ranch. His interest in rodeo developed soon after learning to ride a horse. With some coaching from other ranch cowboys and with daring enthusiasm he began riding saddle broncos in local rodeos. His technique and skill developed quickly. With his competitive nature and determination he resolved to enter the professional ranks.

The rodeo entry fees and travel expenses along with only occasional winnings left the young cowboy with a constant struggle for survival. His persistent love for the sport and the "family" support he received from his friends kept him competing. He traveled from one rodeo venue to the next in his old red Ford pickup. His clothing and meager possessions were stored in a large old Army duffle bag that he carried beside him in the cab of his pickup. There were times when he scarcely could afford more than one meal each day.

Nell's story was quite different. Having grown up on her parent's Oklahoma cattle ranch, she had been riding horses since she was old enough to sit alone atop the pony her father had purchased for her. Riding horses and then becoming involved with barrel racing became a natural for her. During high school her reputation and success in the sport became well- known throughout the state of Oklahoma.

On that summer afternoon in Dodge, Billy Joe Sampson and Nell Crandall became acquainted while sitting together on the ground in the shade of a horse trailer. From that first day, they shared a mutual attraction for each other. For the remainder of that season at each rodeo venue they spent as much time as possible together. Their deeply growing love for each other was a match made in heaven.

In 1954 following a small private wedding on the Crandall ranch they established their first home in a tiny frame rent house a few miles down the old gravel road from Nell's childhood home. Since neither Nell nor Billy had brothers or sisters, the newly married couple were eager to begin a family of their own. Much to their disappointment their wishes for a family never materialized. Their affection was directed to their two small cattle dogs that traveled with them from rodeo to rodeo.

Management and operation of the ranch soon fell upon Nell and Billy due to the advancing age of her parents. This responsibility soon reduced their competition on the rodeo circuit. On a sunny fall day in 1960, Nell's mother, Jayne, suffered a severe stroke. She was rushed to the county hospital but passed away a few days later. It soon became evident that domestic help was needed to assist in the care of her father, Barclay whose health was also failing.

Trudy Kendall, a single young mother was hired to assist in Barclay's needs and to keep up the large two-story ranch home headquarters. Very soon she proved to be a devoted caretaker for Barclay in addition to being a superb cook and custodian for the home. Her presence allowed Nell and Billy time for the management and operation of the ranch.

Jeremy was Trudy's six year old son and when not attending school frequently accompanied her to the ranch each day. He was a handsome and well-behaved little boy with a full head of black wavy hair. He usually wore a broad smile on his face. The boy captured the hearts of Nell and Billy. They looked forward to his visits and for the time he could be with them caring for the cattle and other ranch work. In their minds, Jeremy soon became their little "adopted" son.

One foggy March morning in 1962 while Trudy was driving Barclay to town for his doctor's appointment, her car was struck by a large oil field truck veering across the highway directly into them. Barclay Crandall died at the scene. Trudy was rushed to the hospital where she died of her injuries the following morning.

Barclay Crandall's body was cremated, and like his wife, Billy and Nell buried his ashes next to hers beneath two huge oak trees standing high on a hill in the back corner of the ranch. The Crandall's had issued specific instructions to be followed upon their deaths in addition to establishing Nell and Billy as the sole heirs of their entire estate.

The weeks following the accident were extremely difficult for Nell and her husband. They not only had to endure the grief and loss of Barclay, but now they had an eight year old boy they had come to love as their own and who now had no parents or family to raise him. Little Jeremy was experiencing grief with the death of his Mom and was having difficulty grasping and comprehending its meaning. By mutual decision along with legal consultation and assistance, Nell and Billy Joe Sampson sought and received legal custody of Jeremy Lee Kendall. The Sampson's home became Jeremy's new home. He adjusted quite rapidly to his new surroundings and became close to Nell and Billy.

Jeremy was given responsibilities on the ranch and his new parents disciplined and treated the boy as if he was their biological son. For several years everything went smoothly until an unexpected event occurred in 1968.

Mineral exploration on the expansive ranch brought the discovery of an immense vein of natural gas. Three deep wells with pipe lines were constructed in the following months and placed into operation. Over night Nell and Billy Joe Sampson began to experience a wealth they had never dreamed possible as monthly royalty checks began to arrive.

This sudden and unexpected new fortune brought few changes to their lifestyle and marriage. They remained friendly and respectful as always to their ranch employees, ranching neighbors and friends. They retained both of the Mexican ranch hands that Barclay had employed for many years. With the ranch hands' continued help, Billy Joe managed all the ranch maintenance and Nell assumed full responsibility for the financial aspects of the ranch including the gas well production records. For the first time in their married life they had financial security.

The Sampson's new wealth beginning in 1968 brought a marked change in Jeremy. Until this time, the relationship the couple shared with Jeremy had been warm and happy. It had been a joyful experience for all three in spite of the tragedies each had encountered. The boy had learned a great deal about life on a working cattle ranch and the responsibilities it required. He had received not only love and affection but also encouragement during the difficult period following his mother's death.

Knowing his guardian parents had no other living family members except for himself, the young fourteen year old began some very serious self-inspection. Jeremy reasoned that at some time in the future, it was likely that HE would become heir to the ranch and to the Sampson's estate. All of these thoughts soon developed into a fantasy. On occasions while in town, he would pay a visit to the public library and begin reading books with information on wills, inheritance, and similar subjects. He began visualizing a future life for himself with expensive cars, clothes, and with untold money to spend for whatever and whenever he pleased.

With this developing fantasy brought a change in Jeremy's character and personality. His previous interest in school and the ranch quickly diminished. He began using both marijuana and alcohol. He became belligerent towards both Nell and Billy. With this change in character came frequent encounters and conflicts with teachers, other students, and the law. The Sampson's desperately tried to change his attitude and to reason with the young man whose life they saw spiraling out of control. On more than one occasion Jeremy was arrested by the local police for various problems including petty larceny, drug use, and assault.

In 1972 Nell began planning a special eighteenth birthday party for Jeremy. Just before that day, the young man, without any explanation, gathered up his clothing and personal items from his bedroom and placed them in a cardboard box. While Nell was in town that day, he took $300.00 from her desk drawer and left the ranch driving the two Mexican hands' white ranch truck. After discovering his absence and then his failure to return home or contact them after an extended time, Nell and Billy were both disheartened but yet relieved. For the next twenty years the Sampson's received no word from Jeremy Kendall. His absence and complete loss of communication remained a mystery for them for years.

In early 1992 Nell began experiencing periodic pains in her abdomen along with gradual loss of appetite, progressive fatigue and weight loss. Following extensive medical and laboratory examinations she was given a diagnosis of pancreatic cancer. Exploratory surgery was performed and revealed a poor prognosis. Chemotherapy was begun, but her condition deteriorated rapidly. Realizing her fate, Nell was determined that she should die at home on the ranch. She gave Billy her instructions for cremation and for him to bury her ashes next to those of her parents under the twin oaks. With Billy at her bedside holding her thin pale hand, Nell died at home in her bed one evening according to her own wishes.

For Billy Sampson, on that evening he lost not only his beloved Nell's life but also his own. It would never be the same without Nell. Two days later with a beautiful sunset covering the western sky, Billy saddled his buckskin mare, took a spade and the small square container of Nell's ashes, and rode slowly towards the high hill in the back pasture.

As Billy rode through the silence of the early evening, tears welled in his eyes. Arriving on the hill, he dropped the reins to the ground and dismounted. With care and reverence he dug a small hole into the reddish colored soil beneath the two huge oak trees and tenderly lowered the container of Nell's ashes into its bottom. After covering the small container with dirt, he fell to his knees in a silent prayer to his Master.

The weeks and months that followed were extremely difficult for Billy Joe. He felt Nell's absence in so many places and ways. Now when she was gone their love and happiness they had shared meant more to him than he ever realized. Nell had handled all of the ranch business matters as well as the couple's finances. Billy was at a loss to know what and where to turn. She had kept detailed records on everything. Billy immediately requested the services of their attorney and accountant to assume management of all legal and financial matters for him.

The cowboy's personality and character throughout his life had come from his honesty and the trust he had in everyone he met. He prided himself that anyone could go to the bank on Billy Joe Sampson's hand shake alone. One matter that he insisted upon, much to the discouragement of his attorney, was his keeping a large amount of cash in a small metal fishing tackle box inside the ranch house at all times. The attorney was gravely concerned since the public, knowing of the

Sampson's new wealth, might bring danger for them. Needless to say, Billy did not share this concern.

Maria Sanchez was a young Mexican lady who began working for the Sampson's prior to Nell's taking sick. She had moved into the small guest house behind the headquarters home. Maria kept the large ranch house clean, cooked excellent meals, and was a faithful and loyal nurse to Nell before her passing. The friendly and joyful personality she always maintained was a definite help to Billy after Nell's passing. Maria could cause him to laugh at her off-colored jokes and to smile even when he didn't feel like it. Billy appreciated Maria so very much.

Work on the ranch was handled mainly by the two Mexican hands each day. Having been employed on the ranch for so many years, they were capable of handling any problem that might arise. Both men were excellent workers and Billy continued to pay them well. They had shared an excellent relationship with Billy since Mr. Crandall's death. Billy relied on their loyalty and efforts in keeping the ranch operating in an efficient and productive manner.

After his sudden unannounced departure from the ranch only one day prior to his eighteenth birthday, Jeremy Kendall's life became totally dysfunctional and laced with crime. He gradually became a true sociopath. Without formal education or a high school diploma, he traveled from one job to another never remaining with one for any extended period of time. With little financial means, he frequently turned to crime involving numerous burglaries. Along with his continued use of drugs and alcohol, he developed a lengthy rap sheet with the law in several states. On many occasions he served short periods of time in jail.

Jeremy's personality and addictive habits never resulted in any worthwhile or permanent relationships with women in spite of his rather good looks. On two occasions he had brief, unhappy childless marriages. His wanderlust character took him to several different states where he would settle down only briefly and then move on.

One vexing thought always remained in the back of Jeremy's drug scarred mind. That was his never-ending fantasy for his near certain inheritance of the large Oklahoma ranch which he knew was sitting on top of that huge chasm of natural gas. Sooner or later he was certain it would be his for the taking. BUT - when would that be? If only he knew that answer.

On this particular warm fall night while driving down a Dallas expressway, Jeremy is thinking once again about the Oklahoma ranch and the Sampsons. Since it had been years since he had left, perhaps he should pay them a visit and check on things. He looked at his watch and noted the hour to be nearly 1:30 A.M. He reasoned if he left Dallas now he could be at the ranch early tomorrow morning.

Then he recalled that he had not more than eight dollars in his billfold. This problem would require fixing with a quick hit - perhaps an all-night convenience store. Jeremy began to formulate a plan in his mind. He reached into the glove compartment and pulled out his .44 magnum and laid it beside him on the passenger seat. As his plan raced through his mind, he pulled his car over into the expressway's right-hand lane. As best he could recall there was a large convenient store and gas station about one or two miles ahead on the right next to the freeway exit.

He would pull up to one of the pumps, use a credit card and pump the gas as quickly as possible. Then he would enter the store to purchase a cup of coffee. When ready to pay for the coffee, he would demand the attendant to empty the cash drawer. Anticipating at this hour there would be no customers around, he would grab the cash and be far up the road before the attendant could call the police. If customers were there, he'd find another place.

Ahead, Jeremy noted the exit and the store with its lighted group of gasoline pumps. There were neither vehicles at the pumps nor parked up in front of the store. This fact brought relief as he drove up to one of the pumps. He inserted a credit card and began to fill the tank. When the tank was filled, he hurried into the store with the magnum concealed in one of his pants pockets. Inside, an elderly Asian man stood behind the counter lined with candy and gum and next to a cash register. Jeremy saw no one else in the store.

"Empty your cash drawer on the counter NOW!" he shouted. With that command Jeremy waved the magnum near the trembling man's face. The startled man hesitated at first then responded to a second repeated command from the intruder. He opened the drawer and dumped out its contents onto the counter as instructed. Jeremy grabbed a handful of bills of various denominations and stuffed them into his pocket, while a couple of bills fell to the floor.

At that moment, the attendant started to reach his right hand beneath the counter. Anticipating he was reaching for a gun, Jeremy squeezed the trigger of his magnum with two consecutive shots. The poor man fell violently backwards against the wall and then slumped to the floor behind the counter, mortally wounded. Jeremy bolted out the store entrance onto the drive.

He was immediately confronted by the bright headlights of a Dallas Police patrol cruiser pulling up the drive towards him. The cruiser came to a stop and the officer opened his door and started to get out. As he did so, Jeremy fired two more shots point blank at the officer striking him in his neck and head. The officer fell from the open doorway of his car onto the concrete drive.

Jeremy ran to his car, started its engine, and squealed the tires as he left the station. He accelerated back onto the expressway. Perspiration poured from his face as he tried to embrace what had occurred in the previous few moments. He was now sure of one fact with that full tank of gas – he had to leave Dallas immediately and Texas as quickly as possible.

In the ensuing hours after the discovery of the murders, the homicide division of the Dallas Police Department began an extensive investigation of the double murder. When one of their own is struck down, the investigation that follows becomes even more intense than routine. Such an investigation carries with it a sadness which is experienced throughout the department as well as the entire city. Initial information revealed that the elderly Asian was a Vietnamese who had become an American citizen and had been employed in the store for nearly two years. His family resided in a Dallas suburb.

The dead patrol officer was a 32 year old married Caucasian father of three children. He had been a member of the force for nine years. Both victims were found dead at the scene.

Investigators immediately began a thorough study of the film taken from the store's security cameras for any identifiable information concerning the assailant. The crime scene was studied intensively for fingerprints and ballistic information. The assailant's vehicle was not revealed clearly on the security camera film; however, it appeared to be an older model dark colored vehicle. The in-store camera revealed fairly good vision of a slender Caucasian male appearing to be middle-age and estimated to be 6 feet tall and about 160 to 170 pounds. No other positive markings were evident except that the man appeared to have dark wavy or curly hair. Investigation also included all recently used credit cards at all of the gasoline pumps.

Throughout the remainder of the night the dark blue Ford sedan carrying Texas plates raced into northern Texas, across the Red River, and continued north into the heartland of Oklahoma. Not until after crossing the Red River did Jeremy's nerves begin to settle and his body could begin to relax to some degree. The events that had transpired back in North Dallas played over and over in his mind. He was now mindful to remain extremely cautious and observant in his every move so as not to bring undo attention to himself for any reason.

As he continued driving north, he kept the car radio tuned to a number of different stations seeking any word about the convenience store crime in Dallas. His thoughts now turned for a plan to alter the identification of his auto. Before dawn he must locate some place where he might switch out his Texas plates for those from Oklahoma or some other state. The most logical place would be at a motel where plates could be obtained from an overnight resident's car. This seemed like a necessary plan.

As he was entering the next town, he pulled off the highway and found a Holiday Inn with a number of vehicles parked along one side of the building in subdued lighting. Almost instantly he spotted a car with Oklahoma plates. Having removed the plates from the vehicle, he then proceeded back onto the highway and drove to a more secluded location where he removed his Texas plates and installed the new ones. When completed, he hurled his Texas plates into a deep ravine alongside the highway and continued on his way to the Crandall ranch. With the swap of the license plates, Jeremy felt even more relaxed than he had been for some time.

As the sun was just starting to peek above the horizon of the surrounding Oklahoma ranchland, Jeremy began noticing and recalling landmarks near the ranch. It had been so long since he had been in this area. Many things appeared different, yet there were sites he could clearly remember. Within a few miles, he found the small old wood church still standing on the corner of the Crandall ranch road. Heading east on the road, the entrance to the ranch soon appeared exactly as he remembered it.

By now the sun had risen well above the surrounding hills. It had been a very long night and Jeremy began to feel fatigue and a returning feverishness setting in. He hoped for a brief "hello" to Billy Joe and Nell, and then he could request the opportunity to get at least a brief nap. He drove down the long winding lane and stopped his car on the wide concrete circle drive in front of the spacious two- story ranch headquarters. Nothing appeared changed to Jeremy after so many years, even considering all that new money they had received during the past years.

Jeremy went thru the portico entry and pushed on the door bell. Maria appeared and Jeremy asked, "Is Mrs. Sampson here?" Having never seen this gentleman before, the maid was mystified why he would be inquiring about a person that was dead. She then replied, "Mrs. Sampson is no longer with us so may I ask why you are inquiring about her?"

"She was my Mom for a while and I've been gone from here for many years," Jeremy explained. He then asked, "Is Billy Sampson here?" At that moment Billy Joe came to the door and standing next to Maria looked intently at the man standing before them.

For a long moment the two men stood silently studying one another. Then Billy asked, "Is it possible that you are Jeremy Kendall?"

The young man responded, "Yep, that's me, Billy!" The two men hugged for a rather long moment while tears appeared in the older gentleman's eyes. It had been so long.

"For God's sake, come in Jeremy," Billy demanded excitedly.

For the next hour the two men sat at the large kitchen table while enjoying Maria's breakfast burritos and discussing so many things that had occurred over the years. Finally, Jeremy admitted that with the long all- night trip from Texas, he now needed some sleep. Maria then showed him to one of the guest bedrooms upstairs.

Billy Joe refilled his coffee cup and walked out onto the screened porch, sat down, and tried to comprehend the reason for such a long absence and then such a sudden unannounced visit by the young man. During their long conversation over breakfast, Billy had witnessed what he felt was a very nervous visitor. Billy was profoundly perplexed by the whole scene. Looking out on the drive, Billy saw something even more ambiguous – Oklahoma license plates on the dark blue sedan! The enigma in his mind was why were those plates on the car when Jeremy had stated earlier he had been living in Texas for several years and had just driven from there during the night?

Walking out onto the drive past Jeremy's car, Billy glanced through the passenger door window. Billy was even more dubious when he saw lying on the front passenger floor a .44 cal. Magnum pistol. Billy could see no suitcase or clothing inside the car. Jeremy's unexpected visit was creating more questions than answers for Billy Joe Sampson.

Four hours later, Jeremy awakened and as he lay relaxing on the bed he recalled many experiences during the years he had spent in this house. One thing he especially remembered was the day when he had walked into Nell and Billy's bedroom and saw Billy taking a fist full of bills from an old metal box that was kept under the foot of their bed. Knowing the old cowboy as he did, he'd bet that box was still there with a lot more money in it now than before.

Maria had returned to her guesthouse while Jeremy was sleeping.

After descending the long curved stairway, Jeremy entered the comfortable wood-paneled office and library where he found Billy sitting behind his huge antique desk reading a newspaper. Across the room Jeremy noted the built-in wooden gun cabinet with its glass doors.

Jeremy said, "Boy, a little rest does help." As he said this he sauntered over to the gun cabinet. Inside he could see a holstered .357 magnum hanging on one side of the case.

Not looking up from his paper, Billy asked, "If you live in Texas, how come ya got Oklahoma tags?"

Quick as a flash Jeremy threw open the gun cabinet door and grabbed the .357 from its leather holster. While pointing the weapon at Billy, Jeremy announced in a loud voice, "Gosh darn Billy, I remember that metal box you always kept under your bed. Let's you and me go upstairs right NOW and find it. Whatya' say?"

Jeremy knocked the newspaper from Billy's hands and pulled on his shirt sleeve. Billy rose from his chair and trying hard to show no fear walked to the stairway. Jeremy followed him up the long flight of stairs to the master bedroom, all the while keeping the magnum shoved into the old man's back.

Billy retrieved the old metal fishing tackle box from beneath the foot of the bed. Jeremy grabbed the box and said, "I'll just keep the whole damn thing from now on!" He turned and hastened down the stairs, out the front door, and to his car. He threw the box and Billy's .357 pistol onto the car seat. He started the car and sped down the lane and back onto the gravel road towards the highway.

Billy mopped beads of perspiration from his forehead, rushed down to his office and went directly to his desk phone. He dialed the county sheriff's office and reported the armed robbery, giving a complete description of Jeremy and the fact he was driving an older model blue Ford sedan with Oklahoma plates. He added that he was armed and dangerous. He added that along with him were a metal box with money and a white envelope containing important papers. On the envelope was stamped "Official Copy".

After reaching the highway, Jeremy headed north towards Kansas.

En route down the highway he exceeded the speed limit while passing through a small town. A county sheriff's deputy saw the blue car and gave chase. About a mile distant the deputy pulled Jeremy to the shoulder while he called in the number off the Oklahoma plates. The earlier dispatch from the sheriff's office to all patrol units had been received regarding the robbery. As the deputy left his vehicle, he called for back-up and drew his weapon. With utmost caution he drew up close to the driver's side being shielded in part by the left side of Jeremy's car.

The officer hollered, "Get out of your car SLOWLY all the while keepin' your arms and hands behind your head -- or I'll blow your head clean off!"

Jeremy followed his command, slowly retreating from the driver's seat. The deputy then ordered him to lie facedown next to the pavement while he secured both wrists behind his back.

Moments later a second deputy arrived on the scene. The dispatched information from the sheriff's office matched the description of the person, car, and its contents exactly.

One deputy, after searching the car's interior, confiscated two handguns and a small rusted metal fishing tackle box. With a cloth rag he placed each pistol in individual plastic bags.

He then opened the metal box and counted out ten thousand dollars in one hundred dollar bills. Also in the box he found a tarnished old rodeo cowboy belt buckle and an envelope marked "Official Copy". Upon opening the envelope, he found a folded legal-size paper with the heading "LAST WILL and TESTIMENT" of Billy Joe Sampson.

The Rio Grande Connection

The year was 1988. Enrique and Angelina Frisco were living in a small, run down brown stucco shack on the southern edge of the city of Matamoros, Mexico. Their surroundings consisted of numerous dwellings little better than their own. The unpaved dusty streets were the playground of throngs of children. Either in the front or nearby many of the shacks sat old junked American cars that hadn't been driven in years. Trash littered here and there helped create the neighborhood scene.

Angelina's pregnancy was at or very near term as best she could guess since she had not seen any doctor during the previous four or five years. Recently, walking and just moving around had become more and more difficult for her. The weight of her huge belly was causing her some back pain and her legs and ankles were swollen with fluid.

For some time the young couple had discussed the possibility of leaving this area and crossing over into the States. With a baby soon to arrive, Enrique could find better work and a better salary there. If lucky, he could make enough to send some back to his eighty year old madre (mother) here in Matamoros.

They had purposely delayed any attempted crossing until they were certain the birth of the baby was imminent. Crossing at that time would permit Angelina to have the baby delivered in the Brownsville hospital with American doctors in attendance. Their baby would then be a U. S. citizen, something they were sure would be a great advantage for their child.

Enrique's friends advised him that the safest location for crossing was some distance to the west of the edge of Matamoros. Rarely in that area did anyone come into contact with Border Patrol personnel; however, they urged that their crossing should be at night. His friends also informed him of the hospital's location in Brownsville.

The Frisco's bid Enrique's mother goodbye and with a small bag of clothing and food they left their home for their journey across the Rio Grande and into the United States. It was a warm night with only a sliver of moonlight casting down upon the dry sandy riverbed. While making their way to the opposite bank in Texas, they were joined by several others, all hoping for an opportunity for a better life.

Once across, the small group spread out and disappeared into the dark silence of the night leaving the couple alone. Angelina had become quite tired from the walk and asked Enrique to stop and let her sit down near some mesquite underbrush and rest for a while. They could tell they were near the edge of the town with street lights and houses nearby. Enrique grew concerned that they should be near the hospital before morning light. After a brief rest, the two continued their slow walk into the business district of town constantly aware for the presence of either city police or Border Patrol.

Suddenly, Angelina stopped walking and grabbed her abdomen. A cramping pain struck, and she knew it was the start of hard labor. Since leaving home earlier in the night, she had noticed some pains, but this one was different. Down the street ahead of them they saw the Emergency entrance to the hospital. And then it happened! A sudden gush of water cascaded down her legs onto the sidewalk. Her bag of waters had ruptured. The young woman knew it was time for the baby to be born.

Little Angel Marie Frisco was born inside the Brownsville hospital less than an hour later as the sun was rising over the town. Enrique was joyful and relieved that they had arrived here in the land of opportunity and that his new little muchacha was now an American citizen.

In the weeks and months that followed Angela's birth, the Frisco's lived in a tiny one bedroom second floor apartment in Brownsville. This apartment, although in need of repair, was better than their house in Matamoros. They felt safe there due to the great percentage of Latinos comprising the population within the town and area. Enrique found work with a landscape company and put in long hours seven days a week. His salary was significantly higher than back home. He neglected to register for a green card, yet the company ignored his failure to do so since they found the young man to be a conscientious hard worker.

Angelina found employment cleaning the home of one of the local bankers in town. The banker's wife picked Angelina and baby Angela up in her car once each week taking them to her home. Mrs. Monroe enjoyed having little Angela in her home and enjoyed entertaining her when she was not sleeping while Angelina cleaned her house. At night she would drive them back to their tiny apartment. Angelina enjoyed her time each week working for Mrs. Monroe, and she welcomed the wages she always received in cash. Angelina was told when she started work that a green card wasn't necessary and if a problem ever was to occur that her husband would take care of it.

In 1993 Angela entered the Brownsville School system like all other students in town who were citizens of the State of Texas. By this time she and her mother had grasped the English language quite well. Each shared speaking both English and Spanish at home.

Two years earlier, Enrique left Brownsville after hearing about a higher-paying job up in the Midwest. He regularly sent money back to Angelina and Angela in Brownsville. He applied and had received a green card. He wrote letters to them and talked to them on the phone periodically.

After returning home from school one day, fourteen year old Angela discovered her mother lying on their bathroom floor. She could not arouse her. On the bathroom counter she found a note written in Spanish saying that she was sorry but she couldn't go on any longer. Angelina had taken her own life with barbiturates she had illegally purchased sometime earlier out on the street.

By this time Angela had matured into a beautiful young woman. Her olive complexion, dark eyes, and long black hair accompanied by a striking figure brought attention from both boys and some men considerably older.

Angela dropped out of school soon after her mother's death. Now left alone, she realized she must do whatever necessary to support herself. She had lost track of her father. For whatever reason, he had stopped sending money and letters. Angela believed this might have been the reason for her mother's death.

Being only fourteen Angela could not find permanent employment. What her beautiful precocious body did bring was promiscuity and sexual liaisons with older men. She learned quickly the art of soliciting sex from those who were capable of paying the most. With this newly found income, she was able to maintain a small apartment where she could turn her tricks and purchase the suitable wardrobe to accentuate what God had given her.

Working cautiously on the streets of Brownsville, she became street-wise quickly and with time soon became acquainted with many people that had connections. Angela made friends easily but did not confide her inner feelings and thoughts. She shared these with only a few.

Tyler Jackson was a young man with whom Angela had developed an affectionate and intimate relationship. Tyler had grown up in Brownsville, had gone one year on a football scholarship to the University of Texas, but then dropped out of school for scholastic reasons. He had returned to Brownsville and was working as a bartender in a local restaurant when he and Angela met.

Angela and Tyler developed a romantic relationship over the course of several months. Although intimate, each retained personal secrets in their lives they did not disclose to each other. Angela's venture into prostitution and Tyler's activity dealing with drugs, especially cocaine, were the secrets neither would come to share.

In 2006 at age 18, Angela Frisco learned that she was pregnant. In her previous sexual encounters she had insisted each and every time that the partner must use protection. However, this had not become an issue with Tyler. For the first time in her life, the tall Hispanic beauty had fallen in love. She was excited over the fact that Tyler was likely the father of her unborn child.

Angela shared the news with Tyler. He displayed excitement over the prospects of becoming a father. He and Angela began sharing an apartment and Tyler continued his work in the restaurant. Angela found a job working in a local drug store during her pregnancy. The two shared expenses and developed a happy compatible life together.

Throughout her pregnancy their secrets were never revealed to each other. In 2007, Angela delivered a baby boy that she and Tyler named Brandon Tyler Jackson. A few weeks later Angela and Tyler were married in the home of one of Tyler's wealthy friends. Following the small private wedding, a group of people, all unknown to Angela, arrived for a party.

Angela perceived that many of these people were quite wealthy in light of their fashionable clothing and expensive jewelry. The new bride felt self-conscious and even out of place. Heavy drinking began as the evening progressed – that is everyone except Angela. She declined any drink since she was breast-feeding the baby. Tyler, like his friends, was becoming quite drunk. He escorted Angela around introducing her to "his partners". The entire party was both disturbing and unsettling to the new bride.

The next morning with her husband now sober but with a heavy head, Angela wanted some explanation of who the "partners" were and what Tyler's relationship was with them. With some reluctance Tyler disclosed his relationship with them, and the plans they had made for Angela and baby Brandon!

Since his leaving the University of Texas, Tyler had become involved in a drug ring. The "partners" were members of this ring whose activity involved acquiring a variety of illegal drugs, but primarily cocaine, from the drug cartels across the border in Matamoros. Once having received these drugs, they distributed them to their contacts throughout Texas and the United States.

Tyler's plan for Angela was simple. Two or three times each week she would walk across the bridge spanning the Rio Grande while pushing baby Brandon in a stroller. Arriving at a designated drop location in Matamoros, small plastic baggies of cocaine would be attached to the inside of Brandon's diapers. U. S. Customs would never normally search a baby's diaper for drugs. The two would then return across the bridge. If questioned at the border, Angela's purpose in Matamoros was to visit her aging grandmother who was in poor health.

Tyler told Angela each trip could bring to them perhaps as much as $10,000. or even more. Once she and Brandon got the baggies of the white gold over to Brownsville, the partners' connections in the States assured them a sale.

After first hearing about this plot from her husband, Angela was overwhelmed. If it was true how much money they could receive, she began to give the plan more serious consideration. She finally agreed to try it once. She refused to promise anything after that one time.

One week later the plan was laid out in detail and rehearsed for the first crossing for Angela and baby Brandon. Every conceivable problem that might be encountered was discussed and a solution planned. Angela's dress, her demeanor while walking, her approach and exit from the Custom's check points was detailed and discussed. Tyler imitated Custom's officials on the bridge asking various hypothetical questions. Angela was coached as to what answers she was to give.

On the following morning Angela and Brandon made their first trip. Arriving at the contact point in a filthy old tire repair store in Matamoros, the manager noted the young woman pushing a baby in a stroller. Motioning to Angela, he led her and Brandon into a small office in the rear of the store. Within minutes, Angela placed a clean cloth diaper on her son with nine small plastic cocaine-filled baggies pinned inside the diaper. She then slipped on a pair of infant rubber pants over the diaper. With a light blanket placed over her baby boy, the young mother pushed the stroller out of the building and down the crowded street toward the bridge.

At the U. S. Customs check point, Angela joined at the end of a small line of people, mostly U. S. tourists, returning to Texas. With quiet calm she was motioned through by the agent. The agent smiled at her and commented how cute her baby was. She thanked him and continued on her way. She felt a relief as she entered the United States. Arriving at her apartment she was met by Tyler who rushed to remove Brandon's diaper. He smiled and gave his wife a big hug.

Over the following two months Brandon and Angela made fourteen trips over to Matamoros, each time bringing six to ten baggies back across the bridge. She even became familiar with some of the agents and exchanged pleasantries while passing through the lines of people. The trips had become easy and actually were relaxing.

The fifteenth crossing was scheduled for today. All had gone smoothly for Angela and Brandon as they reached the busy Brownsville intersection just off the bridge on their return. Suddenly, out of nowhere, a speeding car careened wildly through the intersection, and struck Brandon's stroller a glancing blow sending it and the little boy across the pavement and crashing against the curbing. Angela screamed in fright as she witnessed her son being violently thrown onto the sidewalk. She ran to his side crying and screaming for help. The little boy lay motionless while a large laceration on the back of his little head was bleeding profusely onto his shirt and diaper.

A short time later, little Brandon lay on a gurney in the hospital emergency room. Angela was seated outside the room crying hysterically. In preparation for the baby's transfer to the morgue, the ER nurse began removing his clothing. As she unfastened the diaper pins, small bags of white powder fell out into her hands and onto the cart.

Ridin' to the End of the Panhandle Rainbow

Claude T. Rogers had enjoyed a long, hard-working yet simple and enjoyable life. Now as he was approaching his ninetieth year he remained in love with his surroundings where he had lived since his birth. Jacob and Emma Rogers, his parents, had come to this Texas Panhandle cattle ranch soon after their marriage. Jacob was employed as a ranch hand and the Rogers were permitted to live in a small bunkhouse on the sprawling ranch. It was in that little house in 1921 where Claude was born without the assistance of a doctor or midwife. He had spent nearly his entire life up to the present day in this same place.

The Big Gulch ranch had its establishment in the 1800's soon after the end of the Civil War and comprised numerous sections of the rugged and desolate land that help make up the panhandle area of west Texas. Big Gulch's frontier widened out into a tract that extended almost between the tiny town of Channing and nearly to the outskirts of the city of Amarillo. For many folks, this countryside is a total wasteland, but to others it has beauty and serenity produced by its rugged landscape. For "Skeeter" Rogers this was and would always be God's country.

As a very young boy, Claude Rogers received the nickname "Skeeter" from one of the ranch's older hands. The name stuck to the boy like glue thereafter for whatever reason. Few friends or neighbors ever knew Claude by any other name. It's possible in more recent times folks believed it was his given Christian name.

The Rogers family had always been known for their hard work and dedication to the operation of Big Gulch. Their wages earned from working on the ranch had been small through the years, but their conservative, simple Christian life had served them well. They appreciated what they received, and they lived a frugal yet happy and comfortable life.

Growing up here on Big Gulch, "Skeeter" had learned much about ranching and hard work while being around his father and the other cowboys. They taught him how to ride horses, how to rope and fire brand cattle, and all the other responsibilities involved with the operation of such a large ranch. Before entering the nearby rural school, the boy had learned to ride a sorrel mare. "Skeeter" dropped out of school after completing the eighth grade and was hired on as one of the hands. The only time away from Big Gulch his entire life was the three years he had served in the U. S. Army during WWII.

After his return home in 1945, he married his childhood sweetheart, Lilly Barstow, who grew up on a neighboring ranch located several sections down the road but closer to the town of Channing. "Skeeter" and Lilly made their home in one of the small ranch houses on Big Gulch.

She suffered a miscarriage two years later and the young Rogers couple remained childless thereafter. They enjoyed a happy marriage for nearly sixty years. The little cowboy loved his Lilly more than anything in the world! With her creative ability and ingenuity, she provided a warm, cozy and comfortable little home for them.

At age 40, "Skeeter" was thrown from his horse and suffered a fractured hip and knee. His horse had been spooked and bolted away from a large coiled rattlesnake. The rider was pitched onto the sagebrush- covered rocky ground. "Skeeter" was rushed by pickup truck to an Amarillo hospital where he underwent surgery on his hip and knee. After only three months, Claude mounted once again his ranch horse and was back to work. Following this accident he always walked with a noticeable limp, yet the injury never hindered his accomplishing whatever was required on any given day.

Without warning or previous illness on an October morning in 1971, Claude lost the love of his life. Seated at their kitchen table having coffee while her husband was eating his breakfast, Lilly suddenly slumped down onto the table and died with what the doctor assumed to be a heart attack.

In the years following Lilly's death, with progressive disabling complications from his previous injuries "Skeeter" became unable to ride horseback or become involved with strenuous ranch work. He was forced, much to his consternation, to end his work on the ranch. In 1982, he hung up his spurs for the very last time.

With a need to have something to occupy his time, "Skeeter" now at the age of 61, began taking a few lessons in oil painting from an artist neighbor lady. After three or four lessons, "Skeeter" discovered a personal love and hidden talent that he never knew existed. The little bunkhouse he had always called home would now also become his studio. He used the subjects he knew best for his small paintings – cowboys and ranching. Word soon spread of his talent, and neighbors and long-time friends stopped by to see his work. On frequent occasions his paintings were purchased. He welcomed the additional income which supplemented the small Social Security checks he received.

For many years "Skeeter" and Mabel Long had been close friends. Following Lilly's death, the middle-aged wife of one of the ranch hands began bringing by an occasional pie or other dish for the forlorn old cowboy. She frequently attended a few things around his house that she felt a need to be done. "Skeeter" sincerely appreciated her help and all the concern she had for him. He always looked forward to her visits.

In more recent years, with advancing age, "Skeeter" began requiring more assistance in the upkeep of his house and personal needs. Mabel took on a self-imposed guardianship for the old man. With genuine concern for his health and well-being, she began making brief visits each day along with preparing him a warm meal each noon. She had observed his apparent decline in weight and was certain, after looking through his cupboards, he was not eating well.

It was customary for Mabel to drive into Amarillo at least once or twice a month for groceries and other necessities for her husband and herself. This early morning she drove into "Skeeter's" dusty gravel drive and found her friend sitting in his front porch rocking chair enjoying his second cup of coffee.

She hollered to him from her car, "Hey, cowboy, may I get you anything in town? I'm headed to the city, "Skeeter."

The old man pondered her question for long moment and then responded, "Jus' pick me up five lottery tickets. Don't know why but guess I jus' feel lucky today!"

"You got 'em, darlin'. I'll see ya later this afternoon. Don't forget that dish I left in the refrigerator for your dinner!" With that command the loveable little gal stormed down the drive. As he watched her car disappear down the dusty road, the old man smiled and was certain he possessed one of the nicest friends anyone could ask for. Then he wondered out loud, "What in tar nation would I ever do with all those millions IF I did win 'em?"

Around 5:00 o'clock that afternoon Mabel returned from her trip with a sack of groceries, an Amarillo newspaper, and the five Texas lottery tickets for her dear friend. She set everything down on the kitchen counter and said, "Here are a few extra things I thought you needed along with the tickets. Now, don't forget your supper. I'll talk to ya later." And with that, she whirled out the door and was gone.

"Skeeter" removed the food items from the sack and set them on the counter one at a time. He paused while looking at each item as he put them away in his cupboard. He then chuckled to himself, "That darn woman thinks of everythin'." The old man then glanced at the five Texas lottery tickets and their numbers and mumbled, "That was pretty stupid of me buyin' these damn things!"

It was after 10:00 o'clock that evening when "Skeeter's" telephone began ringing while he already was in bed and nearly asleep. It startled the old man, since he rarely had a late phone call. He picked up the receiver and before he could say hello, Mabel's voice was heard, "Darlin' have ya got those tickets so you can see 'em? They just announced the winning numbers on T. V."

"They're on my bedroom dresser," Skeeter answered in a slow sleepy drawl. "I'll get 'em."

Putting on his old wire-rimmed reading glasses from the bed side stand he took up the receiver once again. "I've got the tickets. What's wrong?" he asked.

Mabel shouted excitedly, "Darlin' if I remember right, I think you are now a mega millionaire. Read those numbers back to me NOW!" The old cowboy slowly read the numbers stamped on each separate ticket back to her.

"STOP - that's THE ONE - that's the correct ticket! "Skeeter", honey, you have won a FORTUNE!" Mabel was shouting into the phone. Meanwhile, the old man couldn't begin to comprehend what she had just told him. In fact, it took him several minutes to rethink what she had said. And then the entire matter seemed totally unbelievable.

"Skeeter" tried unsuccessfully to go back to bed, but finally went into the kitchen to brew a cup of coffee. He peered through his glasses at the five tickets spread like playing cards in his hand. The old man then tried to think about what he should do next. This was more than his mind could grasp.

The past two weeks had become a nightmare for him. The quiet life here in his little house along with his paintings had been consoling to him. Word of his fortune had somehow spread and his telephone was now ringing more often each day than it used to ring in a month. His many friends wanted to congratulate him. Newspaper reporters wanted to interview him. "Skeeter" longed to have his quiet days back once again.

Now legal matters required hours of sitting in attorney and accountants' offices in the tall office buildings down in Amarillo. Now it seems that a thousand people have some type of advice for him every day or they have some plea for a contribution or assistance of some kind.

Mabel has remained at his side each day trying to help him during this hectic time. Through it all, their friendship has remained true and lasting. She has asked for nothing and expected nothing from him with the exception of only one thing – and that is that their enduring and loving friendship will always remain and never change.

Author's Postscript

Claude Rogers died two months later. On his death bed he privately instructed Mabel to distribute ANONYMOUSLY his ENTIRE fortune of $85 million dollars to handicapped and poor children throughout the entire Panhandle area of Texas. His only gift to Mabel was a small oil painting, the very last one he had done. But for her, that painting was worth more than a pot of gold. It was priceless!

Ultimate Retaliation

The crash of broken glass from the patio door of Jennifer Banning's ground floor condominium brought the startled and frightened young woman out of a deep sleep. She sat upright in bed while pulling the top bed sheet upward over her chest. It was her custom to sleep in the nude, especially during the warm weather months. She glanced at the bedside alarm clock. The green illuminated dials showed 2:30 A.M. What was about to occur in the following several minutes would become a nightmare the young graduate nurse would live with for the rest of her life.

Her small bedroom was dimly lit, thanks to some of the apartment complex's courtyard landscape lighting just outside the bedroom windows. Immediately, she saw a shadowed figure standing in her open bedroom doorway. The figure threw himself atop his victim and pinned her one arm against her pillow while he muffled her mouth prohibiting her attempted screams with his opposite cupped hand.

Jennifer struggled desperately against his weight and greater strength but with little success. When he rolled off of her next to her side, in a compelling yet quiet voice he said, "Lady, keep your pretty mouth SHUT or I'll kill you!" She resolved to resist his further advances if her life depended on it.

As Jennifer continued in her attempts to free herself from his grasp, with the aid of the dim outdoor light, she noted what she thought was a stocking or something similar stretched over his face and head. With one arm free, she grabbed at the intruder's face. While doing this she tore and pulled away a lady's thin nylon stocking partially exposing his face while the remainder of the stocking remained draped around his neck and back of his head.

This defiant sudden move infuriated her abductor. He reached into his pant's pocket and withdrew a switch blade knife. Jennifer then heard the "snap" when the blade popped open and immediately felt the sharp cold steel pressed into the skin of her throat. That touch brought a lightning flash of immense fear throughout her entire body and left her momentarily paralyzed.

As she lay still for a moment, the intruder suddenly pulled away the top bed sheet exposing her slender naked body. For a brief silent moment he surveyed her beauty and then said, "I know exactly who you are Nurse Banning. You work in the Emergency Room out at the hospital."

"Please don't hurt me," Jennifer pleaded in a whisper.

He continued with a slow deliberate drawl, "Last week you saw me as a patient out there with a cut on my leg. I saw your uniform name tag and remembered your name so I could later look it up in the phone book. The book told me where to find you. Pretty nice place you have here I'd say. Now – it's time for me to have you for myself with nobody 'round!"

Upon hearing this, the woman was now desperately determined to commit to memory everything possible about this crazed man – his body features, speech, clothing, and size. She prayed to God that he would not kill her and that her memory of him might someday help to put him away forever.

Abruptly Jennifer remembered the overhead bedroom light switch on the wall next to the headboard. She always had a dislike for any overhead room lights so she had rarely ever used that switch. With a sudden lurch of her body with her outstretched right arm and hand, she flipped on the switch. The room instantly became brightly illuminated bringing this obtruding villain into clear vision.

"Miss Banning, THAT was a very stupid thing for you to do!"

he shouted angrily and then thrust the knife blade against one of her breasts. With the man now clearly visible holding the knife against her breast, she continued her intensive study of him unheeded by her escalating fear.

He was white, approximately six feet tall, muscular and likely to weigh close to 200 pounds. She guessed his age to be mid-twenties. He wore a dark colored T-shirt and a pair of plaid shorts. Long wavy dark hair partially covered both ears. His face had a smooth complexion and a Van Dyke style, well manicured beard. His nose was somewhat prominent with a slight deformity possibly having been fractured. Partially hidden by his right shirt sleeve was a small colored tattoo. Barely visible, she believed it said - "Mom".

The moments that followed could only be described as brutal and savage. The man stood next to the bed dropping his shorts down to around his ankles. He wore no under shorts so his circumcised member was clearly exposed. As he prepared to mount Jennifer, her fright and desperate attempt to reject him once again took over. It was obvious he had no intention of using any protection. With new found strength and energy, as he fell onto her once again, she began screaming while using both arms and fists, began pounding on his face and head with as much force as she could. At one point she gouged her outstretched fingers into one of his eyes.

Her attacker was now desperate and slashed the 6 inch knife blade deeply across the left side of Jennifer's face and scalp. Blood sprayed out upon the pillow beneath her head. He followed this with four or five deep slashes across both breasts and chest. These wounds brought even more blood onto the grizzly barbaric scene.

As the rapist attempted once again to mount and enter her, his organ remained flaccid which compounded his frustration and anger. The panic-stricken Jennifer saw a contorted, confused expression on his face which was now covered with perspiration that was dripping down across his neck and soaking the collar portion of his T-shirt.

Jennifer's lacerations were not immediately painful due to the shock she sustained, but she soon became aware of stinging sharp pain in her face and entire chest area. Bleeding continued from the multiple wounds, and her body became covered with dark red blood. The bed sheets were soon partially covered with her blood.

Just as Jennifer was about to faint, her attacker abruptly stood erect at the side of her bed, pulled up his pants and ripped off the remnants of the torn silk stocking from around his neck and head. Without any other comment he ran from the room, out through the patio door while slamming it shut as he left. Remnants of glass from the door again fell crashing on the floor.

With him now departed, Jennifer's emotional state brought on a bursting of tears of relief along with the heartache and pain she was experiencing. She stumbled into the bathroom feeling lightheaded and faint. She flipped on the bright vanity lights and while leaning against the counter viewed her ravaged body in the large mirror. What she witnessed in the mirror seemed too unreal for her to believe. She knew she must get help as quickly as possible. She wrapped her body in a large bath towel and her head with a hand towel.

Returning to the bedroom, she picked up the bedside telephone. She had difficulty finding the numbers on the phone through her tear-filled eyes, as she dialed the cell phone number of her fiancé, Eric Johnson. Doctor Eric Johnson was a fourth year surgical resident at the hospital. They had been dating for nearly two years and had begun making plans for their wedding soon after Eric completed his training program.

She and the young doctor shared a late dinner at their favorite Italian restaurant earlier that evening. Eric's call schedule permitted his leaving the hospital for dinner but later was required to return to duty. As she dialed his phone, she was quite certain she could reach him unless he might be scrubbed in for a surgery. Eric answered, only to hear his sweetheart sobbing continuously as she tried explaining the events and horror she had just experienced.

Eric interrupted her excitedly, telling her he loved her and would send the EMS ambulance after her immediately. He then added that he would see that everyone and everything would be ready for her arrival in the ER.

After replacing the phone, with considerable effort she was finally able to pull on a pair of jeans and wrapped fresh clean towels around her chest and head. The dried blood on her scalp, face and chest was uncomfortable but it would have to remain until the ER people could get her cleaned up. She was too exhausted to do anything more.

Within minutes the ambulance arrived and an intravenous fluid drip was begun in her arm. With significant shock and blood loss, her vital signs gave some concern to the paramedics. They transported her quickly to the hospital.

Eric had already notified the police of the attempted rape and assault. They arrived at Jennifer's apartment and immediately established it a crime scene. Eric met the gurney carrying his fiancé as she was wheeled through the glass-sliding entry doors to the emergency department. He grabbed and held tight her quivering hand as she was brought into the large emergency room. Eric was devastated seeing Jennifer's wounds and condition since only a few hours before she had appeared so beautiful at the restaurant.

Waiting in the ER for her arrival, was Dr. Harry Adams, Chief of Trauma Surgery. Monitoring electrodes were attached to observe the nurse's vital signs while Dr. Adams made his initial examination and evaluation. He then gave orders to transfer her immediately to surgery. For Jennifer this would be the first of several surgeries that she would have in the months to come.

It was nearly 7:00 o'clock that morning when Jennifer Banning was wheeled to her private room from Recovery. Eric was at her side observing in surgery and while she was recovering later. She was now responding from her general anesthesia, and asking Eric to explain what had taken place in surgery.

As he looked at her surgical dressings covering a major part of her face and her chest, he told her that the facial trauma was by far the worst and with the delicate anatomical structure damage and the likelihood of scar disfigurement, future restorative plastic surgeries would be required in the weeks and months ahead. Fortunately, the wounds on her breasts and chest had not penetrated into the chest cavity. With time and the plastic closures employed should provide healing, hopefully without disfigurement. Eric then added with a smile, "And sweetheart, your grit, determination and fight with that bastard likely saved your life! Now baby, just rest and remember I love you with all my heart!"

That evening Dr. Adams finally permitted two detectives to enter Jennifer's hospital room to take her statement and to question her at length. With slow deliberate clarity and detail she described the attack from the very beginning to its end. She gave explicit descriptions of the rapist, his demeanor, his physical appearance, and the fact that he ultimately failed to successfully rape her. The detectives made extensive notes of her statement and the answers she gave to their questions.

The police began an immediate man-hunt for the assailant. They called in a female forensic artist to create charcoal sketches of the man. Jennifer's detailed facial description provided significant help in creating the sketches. These sketches were then compared with known rapists and criminals in the area of similar age and description.

During the following two years the scar formation on Jennifer's face required multiple revision and restorative plastic surgeries. Only minor scar revision surgery was required on each of her breasts and chest. Between these surgeries she continued working in the ER. She and Eric agreed to postpone their wedding until she had completely recovered from all of her required surgery. The physical beauty of Jennifer's face and body slowly began to return with the finite surgical skill of her surgeons and with Nature's healing. The rapist was never apprehended. It was presumed he had left the area but the case was never closed.

Today it had been exactly 2 ½ years since the vicious attack on the young nurse. One week from today Jennifer and Eric planned to become man and wife. The wedding plans and excitement had pressed that grizzly terrible day into the back of their minds. Also today Jennifer was having her last day at work until after the wedding and their honeymoon. She had much to get done this next week before the wedding and then it would be a week-long honeymoon in the Bahamas.

Fortunately, this had been an unusually quiet day in the ER. It had given her time to make a long list of things to get done before the wedding. Suddenly, the fading sound of an ambulance siren was heard outside as it pulled into the Emergency drive. With her list pushed to the side, she rushed to the entry. A paramedic hollered, "Caucasian male with multiple gun shot wounds in abdomen!"

The victim was strapped to the gurney with intravenous tubing attached to his right arm. His shirt and pants had been ripped apart by the paramedics. His exposed abdomen revealed two entry sites with a small amount of dried blood around each site. The patient appeared in a coma or deep shock. Monitoring electrodes were attached to his chest. The interrupted wiggle lines tracing across the monitor screen forewarned of the young man's precarious condition. Eric with an Intern rushing behind him entered the room, and the young surgeon placed his stethoscope on the victim's neck over his carotid artery.

At that moment Jennifer whispered in horror, "Oh my God, it's HIM!" Not hearing her, Eric demanded an ampoule of adrenalin. Jennifer turned to the tall red metal emergency "crash" cart standing at her side. She pulled open a large drawer filled with glass ampoules and vials of drugs commonly used in the ER.

Her eyes became riveted not on the ampoule of adrenalin but the glass vial with an entirely different label. Depending on the dosage of THAT administered drug, she knew it is capable of producing nearly instant cardiac arrest.

Jennifer pulled the vial from the tray. She quickly aspirated the entire contents of the vial into a plastic syringe. She then jabbed the needle on the syringe into the auxiliary portal of the plastic IV tubing which was directed into the man's vein. With one quick continuous push, she administered the entire contents of the syringe into the tubing.

Eric was unaware of Jennifer's activity as he watched the wall monitor intently. In a very short while he said solemnly, "He's gone!"

Jennifer responded in a whisper, "Yes, I know."

Barry Draper

The large gymnasium was reverberating with a loud mixture of sounds as the team worked through their last few minutes of practice. The constant "thump, thump" of numerous basketballs mixed with the "squeak, squeak" of the players' Nike shoes on the shiny hardwood basketball floor was a familiar sound for the tall lanky coach standing on the side of the court.

Barry Draper was beginning his twenty-sixth year as the varsity head basketball coach here at Oakview High School. Ever since he could remember, he'd always wanted to be a basketball coach and teacher. Following his playing days at a small state university and receiving his degree in secondary education, he began his career in a small high school in the piney woods area of East Texas.

From his first teaching and coaching days he was certain he was doing exactly what he wanted to do for the remainder of his life. He loved to be around young people and always made a point to conduct himself in a manner that would be a role model for all of his students. After a very successful four years in East Texas, he was hired at Oakview.

Coming to a large city school Barry noted many differences from the small school where he had started his career. The student body was now a mixture of Caucasian, Latinos, and Afro-Americans. There were also a small number of Asian students, predominantly Vietnamese. But for Barry Draper, they were all good kids until they proved otherwise to him. Their skin color made no difference; but it was his obligation

36

to teach them history as best he could and not only be a role model for them but be their friend. This had been his goal since the beginning of his career.

Coach Draper had become not only an excellent classroom teacher but an outstanding basketball coach. His won-loss record at Oakview had brought him requests from several colleges with coaching position offers. The significant increase in salary was certainly alluring, yet he felt a need to continue in a place where he had become very comfortable. The Oakview Board of Education was comfortable with him as well, and it was their desire to keep a real winner for as long as he would stay.

However, five years ago Barry Draper was close to giving up teaching and the job he loved. It was not because he had suffered through a rare losing season, but due to the tragic and shocking death of his seventeen-year old son, Cory.

Cory was an honor student and had been a starter on Oakview's varsity team since his sophomore year. His 6 ft. 5 in. height and basketball skills had won him district honors and visits from college scouts.

On an early warm spring evening five years ago, Cory was sitting on the front steps of his girlfriend's house. Sherrie had entered her house to get each of them a Coke. While in the house, a vehicle sped down the street, and then slowed as it passed the young girl's house. The quiet of the neighborhood was interrupted by a loud gun shot. Sherrie ran out of her house only to see a dark colored pickup speeding away. Cory Draper had been hit in the chest and slumped forward off the steps onto the sidewalk. Sherrie screamed and recognized immediately that Cory was dead.

Witnesses down the street, after hearing the shot, saw the pickup speeding away but were able to get a description of the vehicle and observe the license plate number before it had gone out of site. Police investigation and the witness identification eventually led to the arrest of a sixteen- year old Hispanic member of the "Bloods" gang. During his trial for Cory Draper's murder, it was brought out that his motive was jealousy since, he too, had a romantic interest in Sherrie. The young man was sentenced to 30 years in prison without benefit of parole.

Following the tragic despicable death of his son, Barry Draper suffered a deep sense of grief and depression. He requested a six week leave of absence from school to ponder if he should quit teaching and coaching. Throughout the two week murder trial and for a considerable time afterward, Barry harbored intense anger and hostility towards the gang member who, without provocation, had produced such a profound change in his family. During this absence from school, Barry and his wife sought the seclusion of a mountain cabin in a remote area of southern Colorado.

While fishing one day, Barry was surprised to meet up with a gentleman from New Orleans who was on vacation away from the heat and humidity of the Mississippi delta. The elderly man introduced himself as Doctor Harrison Jenson, a semi-retired psychiatrist. Barry introduced himself to the doctor, telling him that he was a high school teacher and coach in Texas.

This first meeting proved to be one of many that followed for the two men on their vacation. As they became better acquainted, Barry began to relax and share his pent up anger and emotions with his new friend. Dr. Jenson listened intently to the coach's story of his teaching and coaching career and the details surrounding Cory's death. It was a story, sad to say, but somewhat similar to any one that a psychiatrist might hear almost any day in his practice.

The two men's developing friendship and long chats gradually brought about some therapy sessions for Barry. As the days in Colorado passed by, Barry began to lose his anger and his grief was now being slowly diminished. His life now began to have a new meaning. Through the kind old doctor's help, Barry began to realize that he had a mission to accomplish in honor of his dead son. He was determined that his son would not have died in vain.

With the shrill sound of Coach Draper's whistle, the gym once again became nearly silent. The bouncing of the basketballs and squeal of the rubber soles of the team members' shoes on the floor came to a halt. Only the heavy breathing of the players could be heard. The coach walked out onto the court and the fourteen young men quickly gathered around him.

Barry then said, "O.K. men that will be it for today. We had a good practice. I want you to study your play sheets over the weekend. You point guards – remember what side of the floor you come down on each play whether the defense is man- for- man or in a zone. So, go get your shower and have a good safe weekend!"

With his final words, the team members shouted in unison, "GO BUFFALOS!" and scattered running across the gym floor towards the shower room. As they disappeared, Barry drew a big smile on his face. He was pleased with his decision years ago to come back to Oakview High.

The coach entered his office and threw the whistle from around his neck onto his desk. He reached for the phone to call his wife. After dialing his home phone number, he heard it ring a few times then heard Marcie's voice, his wife of nearly thirty years.

"Hi babe! I just finished practice. I'm calling to remind you that I go downtown tonight to check in with the guys. I've got to check on them to see if they're getting their assignments done. I should be home before nine. I'll grab a burger on the way down there, so don't worry about fixin' me any supper," the coach explained.

Marcie then answered, "Barry, honey, please be careful. I'll see you later. Bye."

Barry showered and changed into a faded pair of jeans, an old t-shirt and loafers. Putting on his Texas Ranger's ball cap, he locked his office and hurried out to his car.

Marcie Draper set the phone down. This would be another evening of concern, and yes, even considerable anxiety for her. As she sat down to watch the evening news on television, her thoughts returned to their Colorado vacation following Cory's death. Her husband had returned home with a mission and for the past five years she had witnessed how he had worked so hard towards its end. Tonight was just one part of that mission. The liaisons that he had nearly every weekend since then still always brought her some misgivings, yet she knew this is what he was committed to accomplish.

Barry had learned from his doctor friend that his anger and grief could be converted into a productive venture with the very characters that were responsible for Cory's death. Following his return home from Colorado, the school teacher began his mission by first learning where the "Blood's" territory was located in the inner city. Inquiring at several bars in the territory with the guise of wishing to purchase drugs, he learned the names of the gang's captain and leaders. He also learned, after several visits in the neighborhood, exactly where these young men hung out.

On more than one occasion, Barry Draper's life was threatened by gang members believing he was undercover police. After nearly one year with weekend visits to their territory, the gang's leaders began accepting his presence with them. They learned that he was coming to them and trying to become their friend.

Barry learned to talk straight with the gang members. He placed himself on their level, never trying to appear superior or talk down to them. He used his teacher and coaching experience and skills in organizing street games and with time he began to talk privately with individual members, listening to their problems, and offering advice. The gang members began showing respect and admiration to Coach Barry, as they always called him. The "Blood's" bent on committing acts of crime remarkably began to diminish.

Barry recognized that these young men needed a mentor since many had no fathers. They needed a purpose for living and they needed someone to look up to and love. They also desperately needed a project so they could become productive rather than destructive thus creating some personal pride for each of them.

It had been one year ago this month that the gang's captain and Barry approached an elderly Afro-American widow living in a small rundown wood frame house in the neighborhood. They offered the gang's services to repaint and make repairs on the exterior and interior of the house without any cost to her. With her approval, Barry then contacted several of his business friends who were in the trades businesses for donations of paint, lumber, plumbing supplies, etc.

As Barry approached the old lady's small house this evening, he noted several gang members already there. They came over to his car with smiles on their faces.

"Hi Coach Barry, we're glad you came tonight. Come in the house. We just got it finished and Granny is really happy!"

Getting out of his car, the men followed Barry into Granny's "new" house. She was seated at her small kitchen table. In front of her on the table sat a decorated cake with a frosting inscription,

"To Granny – We love you! From your Boys."

Barry walked through the house and inspected the work the gang members had accomplished. Their work was meticulous and professional in every way. Barry turned to the men and said, "I am very proud of your work. You should be as proud as I am. I know what each of you have learned from this. Now - are you guys ready for my next project?"

There was a resounding shout, "We're ready. Bring it on!"

Identical Difference

Sara Raymond had just been through a long restless night. She had been permitted only brief interrupted periods of sleep due to the physical discomfort associated with her term pregnancy and with her growing anxiety over what the following day would present.

As she opened her eyes, the earliest rays of sunlight streamed through the lacy curtained bedroom window and began to illuminate the room. With effort she raised her swollen body into a sitting position on the side of her bed. Her extra large baggy man's T-shirt was barely stretched over her immense pregnant belly. The small clock on her bedside stand showed a few minutes after 6 A.M.

This was to become a very special day in the life of the young unwed mother-to-be. Her doctor had requested that she report to the hospital at 7:30 A.M. with her elective Caesarean section scheduled for 10 A.M. Previous ultrasound examinations during her pregnancy had confirmed that she was carrying twin boys and that both appeared normal. The elective section was scheduled for today since her office visit and sonogram two days ago had shown her to be at or near 36 weeks gestation.

As Sara arose from her bed and walked into her small bathroom, she removed her night shirt and paused in front of the full-length mirror on the bathroom door and viewed her naked body. She smiled as she noted her rotund round belly and her enlarged breasts, clear evidence of Nature's preparation for motherhood. Following today's surgery, she had hopes that her body would return to the cute slender figure she had always tried to keep.

The warm water from the shower cascaded down over her body and brought an immediate and pleasant relaxation that she needed. It had been a long nine months while she had watched the changes Nature had made in preparation for this day. Within a few hours she would become the proud mother of two little boys.

After drying off, she sat down at the vanity to apply fresh make-up and comb and brush her silky long blond hair. After dressing, Sara took the small previously packed suitcase into the kitchen. It contained articles she anticipated needing while in the hospital along with the carefully chosen outfit she wanted to wear home with the babies.

Out of habit Sara opened the refrigerator door planning to remove the carton of orange juice when she suddenly recalled the nurse's instructions – "Nothing by mouth for at least twelve hours before surgery." She closed the door and then made a last minute inspection of her small apartment to see that everything was in order. This was something she had learned long ago from her mother.

The door bell chimed and Hazel Raymond entered with a huge smile while asking, "Well, baby, are you ready for your big day?" With that question the mother and daughter shared a big embrace. Sara's mother was a petite lady in her late forties with short natural-graying hair. As they had planned, she was going to drive Sara to the hospital and would remain there with her throughout the day. Hazel was as excited as her daughter about the event which was about to ensue.

Hazel Raymond always kept a fresh neat physical appearance with appropriate and fashionable dress whether on the country club golf coarse or in a local grocery store. Her bubbly and lovable personality along with her willingness to help others created many close friendships for her. The modest but comfortable home she maintained was a reflection of her personality.

Following Sara's birth, Hazel always held out hope for the birth of a son. Unfortunately, she was never able to conceive a second time. With this disappointment came a need to give all of her love, affection, and attention to baby Sara and to her husband, Steve. While growing up, Sara and her mother always kept a warm devoted mother-daughter relationship. They were also the best of friends which was evident to everyone who knew them.

Michael Mitchell and Sara Raymond had been sweethearts since their junior year in high school. Mike had two younger brothers and came from a respectable family in town. While in school Mike was a star athlete participating in both football and baseball. He received attention from professional baseball scouts early on, and prior to his high school graduation was drafted and received a substantial signing bonus from the Boston Red Sox organization.

Sara's parents were never pleased with the young couple's long standing romance. Steve and Hazel shared a shrewd ability for evaluating a person's character. Each had a negative opinion of young Mitchell's true character, yet they had always been hesitant to cause any interference - always fearful that it might bring an elopement and marriage that didn't seem right for their daughter. The subtle hints they did drop to Sara simply went unnoticed.

Mike's personality and vanity changed even more with the publicity and notoriety he received from professional baseball. His true colors became evident to Sara's parents, and it became obvious that Michael had become much more interested in his baseball career than any interest he might have in their daughter.

The Raymond's fear and concern became a reality when Sara confided one day to her mother that she was pregnant and that Michael Mitchell was the father. Not surprising to Steve and Hazel, Mike denied any part and suggested that someone else must be the father. However, prior to his leaving town to begin spring training, he had admitted to Steve and Hazel it was possible that he was the biological father. He assured them he would accept his responsibilities. At that time Sara and Mike agreed they would put their marriage on hold and wait for what the future might hold.

From the beginning of their daughter's pregnancy Steve and Hazel remained supportive and brought comfort to her. The unplanned pregnancy was something both had accepted with great disappointment, but they considered it a fact of life and one that they would cope with as best they could.

During the past nine months, Mike called Sara on only two occasions. Each time the conversation was brief and he hadn't inquired about Sara's progress or her feelings. He offered no financial support or gave any commitment to marriage. He had expressed no interest in the two babies he had fathered.

At Sara's request, after receiving legal advice and assistance, Michael Mitchell signed off for having any future rights or custody for the children. They were to receive the Raymond name following their birth. With this matter resolved, Sara relinquished any thought of a future relationship with Michael. Sara made plans for becoming a loving mother along with the continued and welcomed support provided by her parents.

Steve Raymond's graying hair belied his forty-nine years. His athletic build was maintained over the years with daily early morning workouts and special attention to his diet. His good looks along with the fact of his being a varsity basketball player at the university had won the heart of the cute little coed, Hazel Jones. They married during Steve's senior year just prior to his receiving his degree in petroleum engineering.

Following his graduation, the Raymond's moved into a tiny, cheap apartment in Midland, Texas where Steve was employed by a major oil company. With the oil boom under way, the young engineer had climbed rapidly up the corporate ladder. With economic changes from time to time that always seem to occur in the oil business, Steve's loyal dedication to his job kept him employed and a valued employee over the years.

As they drove across town to the hospital, Hazel told Sara that her Dad had left earlier this morning on a business trip to Aruba, but that his love, thoughts and prayers would be with her during this special day while she brought him two grandsons. "He also said to tell you he would call you at the hospital this evening," she added.

In the hours that followed, Sara's elective surgery went as planned. Timothy John Raymond was born at 10:22 A.M. and weighed 5 pounds 10 ounces. Tony Keith Raymond was born four minutes later and weighed 5 pounds 6 ounces. From the moments of their entrance into the world the facial and body likeness was truly identical with the exception of a tiny brown birth mark on the upper left thigh of baby Tony which was the only distinguishing difference between the tiny infants. Each had a heavy mop of dark hair and both gave some resemblance of their father – wherever he might be at the time.

As the days and months passed following their birth, Sara devoted her undivided attention and love in the care of the two babies. Grandma Hazel received pride and joy assisting in their care whenever and wherever it was needed. Providing care for the boys gave Hazel the opportunity she had hoped to have years before but had never achieved.

When Steve's business travel schedule permitted, he spent as much time as possible with Tim and Tony always trying to provide a father figure for them. Rarely did he return home from a trip that he didn't bring a new toy of some kind for his grandsons who had become the pride of his life.

After the twins started school, Sara obtained a secretarial job in a large law firm in the city. She welcomed the change of pace, the opportunity to meet people, and to have an income which permitted her to become less dependent on her parents. Tim and Tony enjoyed school, made many friends, and retained their identical looks which brought problems for their teachers nearly every day.

By the seventh grade, a change began to appear in the boys' relationship with each other. For whatever reason, Tony developed a defiant and aggressive behavior. He became more distant and began to lose interest in school. He had outbursts of defiance both in and out of school, and became argumentative with his mother, brother, and his grandparents. Rarely did a day pass without Tony having a problem with someone.

While in the eighth grade Tony stole several small items from a sporting goods store and was apprehended by the store manager. Steve and Sara met with the store manager and resolved the problem without juvenile charges being filed.

Tony's defiant personality continued during high school. He became involved with a small gang of boys which brought about the regular use of marijuana and alcohol. His grades in school were marginal at best. Sara frequently received telephone calls from school officials regarding her problem son. Both verbal and physical struggles between the brothers became commonplace and kept the household in constant turmoil and unrest.

One night prior to the twins' sixteenth birthday, Tony, along with three of his friends, became involved in a break-in and attempted burglary of a gas station and convenience store. The four boys were arrested by police and taken to jail where they remained over night. The following day, Sara's law firm attorneys had the charges dropped against Tony on a legal technicality.

During these tumultuous years, Tim was a model citizen and student. He excelled in athletics and was an honor student. The actions and problems of his twin brother frequently brought embarrassment and shame for Tim. He always remained close to his mother and grandparents. Following graduation he planned to attend the local Junior College for two years and then enter the Police Academy. His ultimate professional goal was to become a Texas Ranger.

Sara's life raising the two boys had resulted in something much different than what she had expected. There had been occasions when she secretly feared to be around Tony. He had never physically abused her although on one occasion he had threatened her with a kitchen knife. She had kept this a secret from everyone. It had remained a mystery why the twins had become so estranged.

Following high school graduation, as might be expected, the brothers went their separate ways and rarely ever spoke to each other. Sara once heard a rumor that Tony was employed in the San Antonio area by a trucking company. A year later he called one day asking her for money and stated that he was then living in the Galveston area and was out of work. He said he was sharing an apartment with a night club stripper.

Similar calls came on other occasions, always with a hard luck story and a request for money. Sara refused these requests for money each time. It became a horrible case of "tough love" for her to endure.

Tim completed his two years of college and was accepted into the Police Academy. Later he graduated with honors and with self-esteem was a happy rookie police officer. After leaving the Academy, he was employed by the Houston Police Department as a patrol officer. After spending nearly two years on the force, he met and married Judy, a beautiful Rice University graduate from Beaumont, Texas. Judy and Tim purchased a small house in Houston. Soon they were joined in their little home by Ben, a black Labrador pup.

Tim had never received any form of communication from his brother for several years. He was unsure where Tony might be. But knowing his twin brother's personality as he did and what road his life had taken, the young police officer feared the worst for him wherever he might be.

---------------O---------------

It was a rainy, chilly and gloomy night in mid November. Tim gave a tender parting kiss to Judy, hugged Ben, and left their house for the drive to his station in downtown Houston. His patrol shift tonight was from 11 P.M to 7 A.M.

Since before their marriage, Judy had always experienced an uncomfortable nervous feeling when she saw Tim leave for his shift. She kept hoping these thoughts would leave her with time but they never did. She was always consoled when she would see him walk through the door later. The young wife kept reminding herself that Tim was doing what he loved, and she must always keep that fact in mind.

Following Tim's arrival at the station, he changed into his uniform while sharing comments in the locker room with fellow officers about that evening's NBA basketball game between the Rockets and Dallas Mavericks. Joining in the conversation was Tim's patrol partner, Bill Clark. Tim and Bill had been the closest of friends since the day each had joined the Houston department. Each officer had always covered the other's back and each was prepared to lay down his life for the other when and if that became necessary.

When both men were dressed, they received the customary evening report and then walked out to their cruiser parked in the station lot. On this night Bill jumped behind the wheel and drove their patrol car slowly out of the lot, turned left and headed down the rainy street. On the car radio Bill called in to the dispatcher reporting that their unit was underway. As Officer Clark readjusted the radio frequency and settled back into his seat, he commented, "Sure the hell is a cold messy night. Sure hope it stays quiet."

Tim answered, "Me too, but ya know what – this is the perfect night to be at home by the fire with your wife and dog cuddled beside you and watching an old John Wayne movie."

At that moment, the police radio cracked loudly with the dispatcher reporting for all units in the vicinity of 300 South Elysian Street to respond for a robbery in progress. With their location only about six blocks away, Bill flipped on the car's emergency flashers and tromped hard on the accelerator. The police cruiser raced forward screaming down the rain-slick city street. Traffic on all streets was unusually light at this hour perhaps helped by the constant heavy rain that had been falling since rush hour.

As the officers' cruiser approached the intersection of Elysian and Lyons they saw their back-up unit screeching to a halt crossway of the intersection with their emergency lights flashing. Their spot light and headlights were directed across the intersection toward a tall stone building on the corner.

As Bill was bringing his car to an abrupt halt next to the curbing, Tim was already withdrawing his weapon from its holster. Swinging his car door open he leaped out onto the wet sidewalk. He ran up next to the corner of the building and peered cautiously around its edge into the subdued light of the adjacent street.

At that moment Tim saw a figure running directly toward him in the partial darkness. Tim screamed, "Houston P. D. – STOP or I'll shoot!" Two loud gun shots – pop, pop – rang out with the metal jackets striking the concrete cornice of the building immediately above Tim's head.

Again Tim yelled out, "Throw your gun down – NOW!" This command was followed by a third shot from the suspect. Tim then wheeled around the edge of the building in a semi-crouched position firing three consecutive shots from his 9mm Glock service revolver. He heard a loud moan and then witnessed the dark figure slump forward face-down into the curbing-deep water only a few feet from him. Tim holstered his weapon.

Immediately, Bill and the other two officers arrived with weapons drawn. Bill's flashlight was directed upon the body lying in the street gutter. The officers noted a dark ski mask pulled over the victim's head. Tim crouched down, turned the victim's head to one side, and pulled up the mask exposing his face.

The victim's face was one only too familiar to the officer and one he never would mistake in identifying. Tim turned away with a wave of nausea passing through his body. He slumped to his knees in the rushing water flowing along the curbing.

The night was very black and silent once again. Only the heavy loud sobbing of Officer Timothy Raymond could be heard. The chilling rain continued to fall upon the four police officers and upon the motionless body lying at their feet.

Following the Weather Pattern

It was nearly 10:45 P.M. when Tina Nabors walked out the side door of the Channel 3 KWHN television studio building and into the personnel parking lot. The tall blond haired former runner-up for Miss Texas had just finished giving her weather report in conjunction with the 10:00 o'clock News broadcast.

As she walked across the brightly lit parking area towards her car, she tapped the "unlock" button on her key chain. The front and back lights of her new BMW turned on in response. She glanced out across the city skyline with all of its lights illuminated against the darkness of the mid-summer night sky. The view was spectacular. Tina had just reported on the news that the current temperature remained in the high eighties at this time of the evening. After being inside the air-conditioned broadcast studio, the warm night air felt good to her.

She opened the driver's door on her flashy black on black coupe and settled into its soft plush leather seat. The smell of newness had yet to wear off inside the car. Before starting the engine, Tina slipped off her fashionable suede pumps with their three inch heels. Her aching feet had requested she drive home tonight in her stocking feet. As she adjusted her seat belt and backed out of the parking space, she felt exhausted and was ready to get to her condominium and relax.

Fifteen minutes later Tina turned off the expressway and down the tree-lined boulevard and continued on to the gated front entrance of her condominium complex. She waved at the security guard as he permitted her entrance through the gate. She pulled the car into a vacant space in the resident covered parking area just outside her building.

Gathering up her pumps and large shoulder-style leather purse, she got out and popped the lock on the doors. Walking stocking - footed up the warm concrete walk through the portico she removed the front door key from her purse and unlocked the door. Reaching inside on the side wall, she flipped the switch turning on two large end table lamps in the spacious living room. It was good to get home. Since moving to this city only one month before, she was pleased with this condo, especially since it was now furnished like she wanted and the fact that she's finally gotten settled in.

Once inside, she threw down her heels and purse on a chair and made a brief visit to the bathroom. She walked towards her small gourmet kitchen, but then noted the small red-flashing light on the desk phone in the hallway. After pushing the small silver button on the receiver, came the recorded sound of that tormenting man's voice that she had been hearing numerous times in the past two or three weeks.

"Hi Tina. It's me, baby. Boy, you certainly looked plenty sexy in that yellow outfit you were wearing today when I saw you eating lunch with that other gal!" the voice recording said. Tina quickly pushed the stop button followed by the erase button. Her condo became quiet again as Tina stood trembling next to the phone.

These harassing calls had not only become a nuisance but with their increasing frequency were making the young woman very uneasy and even fearful. It seemed to Tina the voice was that of an older individual rather than a younger person. What was most bothersome was the fact that this creep had somehow obtained her unlisted house phone number, a phone she rarely used. She routinely used her cell instead. She reasoned if he could get her unlisted home phone number wouldn't it be possible for him to locate where she lived? She tried to erase that from her mind.

Tina hurried into her bedroom, changed out of her clothes, and slipped on her favorite thin, skimpy night shirt. She entered the small kitchen, poured a glass of Merlot, and returned to the living room where she turned on some soft music on her favorite local late- night easy-listening FM station.

Curled up on her plush white fabric sofa, she began to analyze the many phone recordings she had received. For some reason this character had her targeted within the brief time she had lived in and been employed as one of Channel 3's weather personalities in this city.

She had not dated anyone since moving here. The only men that she had become acquainted with were fellow employees of KWHN. With the exception of three or four members of the camera crews all were married as far as she knew. Here in the complex, she had only a nodding acquaintance with her neighbors. During the past few weeks she had been extremely busy both at work and in settling her condo. There simply had been no time for any social life.

With tonight's call, this guy obviously was in Julio's Mexican restaurant when she and Sandy were having lunch. Sandy Carlson, her new and closest friend, had become acquainted the second day after Tina started work at the station. Sandy was a television reporter out on the street for Channel 3 covering breaking news, or any other assigned news story she was asked to cover for the 6:00 and 10:00 P.M. News broadcasts. She was a really cute and sharp gal. She always had her ear to the ground.

Tina's thoughts returned to the facts. Yes, she was with Sandy at Julio's this noon and yes, she was wearing her yellow suit. Tina wondered out loud, "I'll bet he even knows I had chicken enchiladas." The tall glass of Merlot was starting to help her relax. She set the glass down on the coffee table, walked into the bathroom and removed her make-up and brushed her teeth. In spite of her concern, sleep followed soon after she crawled into bed.

The following morning as was her custom, Tina flipped on the remote to her bedroom television to get the local news and weather before rising. Her thoughts once again returned to a problem she had never dreamed possible. As the early morning show flashed across the screen, Tina began to contemplate the entire situation facing her.

The REAL fact was Tina Nabors, in only one month, had become a celebrity in this city and within the local viewing area - like it or not. With her imposing face on the television screen several times each day the public was viewing her as someone special and even to some sick individual - enticing. The viewing audience might then fantasize as either loving or hating her, depending on the person.

The following day at the station for the first time, Tina finally confided with Sandy about the phone recordings and the fear that she was now beginning to experience. Tina felt some comfort just having someone with whom she could share the ordeal.

Sandy responded with, "Well, so far it's only stupid phone calls. You have no information or identification to report to the police for obtaining a restraining order. In fact, at this point in time he really hasn't stalked you. Nevertheless, out on the beat I'll certainly keep my ear to the ground since I come across some pretty goofy folks from time to time."

Two weeks passed with no calls which made the young celebrity begin to feel her admirer had given up or left town. She began to relax and settled back into her daily work schedule and routine.

One afternoon on her way to Channel 3, she pulled into a gas station for fuel. She was filling the tank when directly across from her she recognized the man who worked as a security guard at the condo complex front gate. He was not dressed in his usual white shirt and dark tie uniform. As Tina continued to pump the gas, the man approached her and asked in a soft voice, "Aren't you Channel 3's Weather lady I see each night on television?"

Tina hesitated and was afraid to reveal her identity, but then said, "Yes, you're correct." She feared what his next comment might be.

He then added boldly, "I note on your left hand that you're not married. I'd be most happy to invite you out to dinner some evening when you're not working. Could we arrange such a thing? I also know you are new in the city and I would be more than happy to show you around."

Tina shut off the gasoline entering her car, and began getting into her seat. Turning to the man she responded coyly, "Thank you but my fiancé wouldn't approve!" She started her car engine and drove out of the station. She smiled as she drove down the street quite proud of her impetuous thinking and untrue response. Now knowing that this guy worked for the apartment complex, she was certain she had not heard the last from him. Little did she realize how true her intuition was.

Driving home that evening from the station, Tina's thoughts flashed back to her unexpected afternoon encounter with the security guard. She guessed him to be nearly as old as her father. This guy was starting to give her the creeps. Then – it struck her like a bolt of lightning!

Could this character be responsible for the phone recordings? It all began to make sense to her. He knew precisely her daily work routine. Each evening she normally passed through his gate about the same time. The complex management office had on their records each tenant's unit number, both home and cell telephone numbers, their place of employment – AND – a master key for each unit for the management's emergency entrance if and when it might be required.

As she approached the entry gate her plan was not to speak to him or acknowledge him in any way. As she pulled into the entrance drive she noted the security guard house lights were on as usual BUT the creep wasn't inside or anywhere to be seen nearby. Tina was baffled when she then observed the metal entrance gate bar was in the permanent up position.

The entire scene was unusual and simply didn't add up. For a moment she thought she might be assuming a great deal. Perhaps the guard merely had to leave for a time to go to the bathroom. Her thoughts raced back to everything that had happened in the past weeks and to Sandy's comments. Then she recalled the bold advance he'd made that afternoon.

This guy was stalking her and she must do something about it! She pulled the BMW over next to the curbing immediately inside the gate and shut off the motor. Reaching for her cell phone she dialed "911" and reported her location and that she needed a police officer escort into her condo. She told the 911 operator of her fear of a stalker whom she considered might be dangerous. She also added that a security guard at this moment was not around.

Tina waited only a brief time while seated in her car with the car doors locked when a patrol car pulled into the entrance and stopped next to her car. The officer came over to her car and Tina identified herself saying that she had made the 911 call and the request for assistance. She then briefly told the officer her story. He listened intently as she told of her suspicion especially now that the guard wasn't in his customary location.

The officer then followed Tina to her customary parking area and then on foot to her front door. By this time suspicion had arisen in the officer's mind after hearing Tina's story. Prior to unlocking the door, the officer whispered to Tina, "I must enter first. I want you to stay here outside on the entry until I search your apartment. I'll let you know when to come in. O. K.?" Tina informed the officer of the light switch just inside the door on the right and acknowledged that she understood his instructions.

Taking Tina's key, the officer unlocked the door and entered quietly, all the time remaining in the dark. A voice came from within the dark interior, "Tina, darling, I knew you'd be coming home soon. I found your wine in the frig. I've poured you a glass. Come in now and you and I will have a delightful evening together."

The police officer then turned on his flashlight and directed its bright beam towards the sound of the voice while also finding the light switch on the entry hall wall. After flipping on the light switch, Tina's living room became fully illuminated revealing a middle-aged, obese man sitting in one of Tina's arm chairs. He was startled to see the tall city police officer facing him in the room. Lying on the carpet next to the man's feet was a new roll of clothes line rope, a large roll of duct tape, and a hunting knife.

Chico

"Don't hit Momma again!"

"Shut up Chico!"

With that loud command the tall black man struck his small son with his open hand across the side of the boy's head. The blow knocked the boy onto the kitchen floor. Felicia O'Neil wiped the tears from her swollen face and dark eyes as she tried to get back onto her feet. The blows she had received from her drug-crazed and drunken husband had produced a severe headache. She was determined to protect her son.

This scene had been repetitive over the past several months, and always followed sometime later by remorse and meaningless apologies. Each time Felicia tried desperately to forgive in hopes that things might change.

O'Neil's reside in a small, two bedroom frame house at the edge of Bender, a small ranching community about eighty miles northwest of Dallas. The exterior of this rent house has been long overdue for a new paint job. Both the front and back small yards have overgrown grass and weeds and need care. In the narrow gravel drive sits a rusted out 1972 Ford 150 pickup with all four of its tires flattened. At this moment, behind the pickup Robert O'Neil has parked his most cherished possession – a maroon 1983 Cadillac Coupe de Ville.

After ending his tirade, Robert rushes out the back door all the time cursing and jumps into his car. He revs its engine loudly and then squeals the rear tires creating a cloud of dust as he leaves. Felicia embraces Chico for a long moment.

Felicia met Robert O'Neil nearly seven years ago at a Willie Nelson concert at Fort Worth's famous Billy Bob's honky tonk. On that summer night he grabbed at her heart strings and she never let go. Within her Latino heritage, up to that time, she had never found anyone that she could love. The tall, well-built, handsome black man with his sparkling brown eyes and small thin mustache had smitten her from that first night listening to Willie.

After a brief courtship they were married in Fort Worth with blessings provided by a Justice of the Peace. Felicia's mother had misgivings about Robert from the start and had much preferred that her only daughter would marry one of their ethno. Felicia was nearly twenty and Robert was twenty-two.

Soon after their marriage, Robert's explosive temper began to appear accompanied with verbal and occasional physical abuse of his new wife. He could rarely keep steady employment due to altercations with fellow workers on nearly every job. He was always quick to lay the blame on someone else. The couple could never rely on any steady income from Robert. Felicia found employment in a 7-11 convenience store and with her meager but steady salary, she provided their rent and food money.

Felicia wanted a baby and convinced herself that having a child would give her husband a new focus and a reason to obtain a steady job. Robert, however, never shared Felicia's family interests. His "family" was a small group of "bros" down on the east side of Fort Worth. They provided Robert with companionship and a mistaken sense of power.

While reading the newspaper one day, a classified advertisement caught Robert's attention. It read:

WANTED –Dependable male in good health for employment at Granite Construction Company, Bender, Texas. Excellent salary offered. Contact Jed Daniels at (916) 842-6166.

Robert had no notion where Bender might be, in fact, he'd never heard of the town. His friend, Marcus had heard of it saying it was about 70 miles north of Fort Worth. Robert called the Granite number, was given an interview date and time as well as directions. Robert and Marcus quickly made big plans for a road trip to Bender. With a chance to make BIG money, Robert was already making equally BIG plans. He could already see himself standing in a Cadillac dealership showroom deciding which one to order.

As the two friends drove north in Marcus' old Buick Regal with its 168,000 miles on the odometer the car radio screamed with jiving bop music. Each man sipped their Coors Lite between puffs from the joints Robert had brought along for the trip. An hour later they saw the exit sign – BENDER

Pop. 5008

Gulping the final swallows of his Coors, Robert pitched the empty can out his window while reaching in his shirt pocket for the scrap of paper with the directions to the company office. He suddenly remembered that Granite's Mr. Jed just might be one of those Baptist teetotalers and might smell the Coors and joint on his breath. He removed the wrapper from a stick of Dentyne and popped it into his mouth for insurance.

O'Neil felt the interview had gone well. In answering several of Daniel's questions he was forced to alter the truth somewhat – actually to drop a few lies on related questions about the use of drugs, alcohol, or previous DUI's.

While Robert was having his interview, Marcus was driving around town scouting for a place to purchase a cold six-pack of Coors for the return trip home. Much to his surprise, he finally learned that Bender was in a dry county. He returned to Granite and found Robert waiting outside for his return.

As they pulled back onto the highway, both men agreed a stop in some town across county lines was needed to take a good pee and get some Coors Lite. Their needs were fulfilled several miles later with a stop at a convenience store in a small town.

Two days later Robert called Granite and was informed that he would be hired. With excitement, Robert accepted Daniel's offer and a starting date in two weeks were agreed upon. Now it was time to move from Fort Worth to Bender.

For as long as she could remember, Felicia had never seen Robert so excited and happy. He told her it was time for a celebration that he was about to start making some BIG money. He rushed to the phone to request delivery of a large-size Domino's pizza with everything on it! Felicia couldn't help but be excited with Robert's happiness and with their pending move. She called her mother to share the news.

All of these thoughts came back to Felicia on this day as she sat here in the little kitchen after the beating she and Chico had just received. She sipped deeply from her cup of coffee hoping it might help relieve her throbbing head. Yes, it had been a good move, coming here to Bender and renting this little house. For a time everything had gone well. Then Robert returned to his past behavior and habits. For the past six years she at least had Chico to provide her some sanity and love.

Felicia's thoughts then raced back to that terrible night here in this kitchen when she informed Robert of her pregnancy. She recalled how carefully she had planned this to be such a special evening for them with Robert's favorite meal, a bottle of wine, tablecloth and candles. Then she remembered his violent reaction upon hearing the news. She recalled how he had jerked everything from the table onto the floor. It proved to be a clear indication of what was to become of their relationship. That was only the first of so many nights that she had cried almost the entire night before finally falling to sleep.

Then she remembered how Sonya, her closest friend in Bender, had taken her to the hospital when she was in labor just prior to Chico's birth. For a few moments, following his belated hospital visit, Robert and she finally agreed on a name for their son.

Following little Chico's birth, her life had changed forever. Since that day, Robert spent progressively less time at home and with only infrequent brief visits. These visits brought arguments, misery and frequently assault upon herself and sometimes on Chico just like this morning.

When Chico was quite small, Felicia began reading to him each day and began teaching him words in Spanish. She hoped that he would become bilingual. Along with her teaching, she discovered Chico's artistic talent. With his continued interest in drawing pictures she has always kept him supplied with pencils and paper tablets. Her refrigerator door has always displayed his latest and best drawings.

Felicia glanced at the kitchen wall clock and realized it was nearly noon. After Robert left this morning, her mind was preoccupied with memories and daydreaming. Oh, how much she wished for a change for herself and her young son. She began preparing Chico's favorite lunch of macaroni and cheese with a dash of Mexican salsa. Having no appetite she would settle for a warmed-up tortilla. Chico had remained closed in his small bedroom all morning.

Chico entered the kitchen and Felicia looked lovingly at her son. The boy had received many of his father's facial and body features. His skin was much lighter and very similar to her coloration. The mixture of Robert and her ethnic genetics had produced a very handsome little boy.

Before Chico sat down to his lunch, they heard a sharp loud knock on the front door. Felicia dropped her tortilla and rushed to the door. After opening the door she was confronted by a tall rather heavy-set county sheriff's deputy. She noted his cruiser with motor running and emergency lights flashing outside in the drive.

The deputy then asked, "Are you Mrs. Robert O'Neil?" Still somewhat bewildered by his presence, Felicia replied, "Yes, I am Felicia O'Neil and Robert is my husband."

With some hesitation the deputy then said, "Mrs. O'Neil, I'm very sorry to inform you of this but a person we believe to be your husband is dead." Upon hearing this Felicia collapsed back into one of the living room chairs.

The deputy continued, "Approximately 9:30 this morning a gentleman believed to be Robert O'Neil, your husband, entered the downtown bank armed with a gun and carrying a small gym bag. While others in the bank watched, he ordered each of the bank's three tellers, one at a time, to empty their cash drawer into his bag. He then exited the bank and started to enter an older model maroon- colored vehicle parked outside the bank with its motor running. Upon seeing a Bender police officer approaching on foot, the suspect fired shots at the officer. The officer was not struck, but responded by firing two shots. The suspect died instantly at the scene. Mrs. O'Neil, the coroner has requested the victim's body transferred to the hospital for the inquest and autopsy. I have been requested to escort you to the hospital so that you might provide our department with a positive identification. We need to go there now."

The deputy then asked, "Is this your son?"

Chico answered immediately, "Yes, my name is Chico Allen O'Neil."

The deputy escorted Felicia and Chico to his cruiser and directed them into the rear seat. After turning off the flashing overhead emergency lights, they proceeded to the Bender community hospital. Upon arriving there, he escorted them through the front entry and into a large reception area. The small, well-equipped 50 bed hospital, originally built in the 1950s, had been well- maintained and had served the community well through the years since.

In the reception area they were met by Mary Jacobs, the day 7-4 nursing supervisor. After introducing herself, she said, "I'm sorry to meet you under these circumstances, but I'm sure this deputy has explained to you their need for you to make a positive identification for them. This should not take long. I do believe it best that the boy remains here." Chico offered no protest and sat down in a nearby chair.

Felicia and the deputy were then led down the corridor; finally stopping at a large door with a small sign attached which read "Morgue". The nurse removed a key from her uniform pocket, unlocked the door, and reached inside to switch on the small room's bright overhead lights. After entering, the heavy door swung shut and self-locked behind them.

Felicia was immediately struck by the pungent odor of formaldehyde something she had never experienced. She then made a brief visual survey of the entire room and then focused on the long stainless steel table in the center of the room on which lay a body completely covered by a heavy large white sheet. A surgical lamp was suspended from the ceiling directly over the table. A large steel sink was attached to a wall next to the table with a long rubber hose joined to its faucet. Nearby, also suspended from the ceiling, was a pan scales. The wall on the opposite side of the room had a counter and a series of glass fronted cupboards. Everything was clean and almost sterile in appearance.

She felt a cold chill pass through her body as her eyes became fixed on the table in front of her. After permitting Felicia a few moments to acclimate to the surroundings, Nurse Jacobs then asked quietly, "Mrs. O'Neil, are you ready?" Felicia nodded and Jacobs then slowly and reverently withdrew the drape downward exposing the upper half of the body beneath.

Tears welled in Felicia's eyes as she viewed the lifeless body of a man she once so long ago had so madly loved. The same body was the person just this very morning she had hated so much. Robert's body was fully clothed exactly as she'd last seen him this morning. A large dark blood stain now covered a large part of his faded red plaid shirt. In the upper left side of his chest, Felicia could see two separate holes where the fatal two slugs from the officer's weapon had tore into the shirt fabric. Peering intently at Robert's face, Felicia almost believed she could detect a smirk - or was it a partial smile?

Felicia turned away from the table saying in a near whisper, "Yes, that's Robert O'Neil – now may I please go?" Back in the patrol car, Felicia sobbed quietly and dabbed a crumpled well-used tissue at her reddened eyes. They were soon home and she thanked the deputy for his kindness as he helped her and Chico from their seat.

Shortly after the deputy left, Sonya arrived to be with Felicia and help in any way possible. Felicia stood silently in the kitchen peering at nothing in particular out the window into the back yard. Shock, sadness, and relief were a mixture of emotions that now filled her mind as she stood there. She was convinced the Lord would care for Chico and his mother in the days and years to come.

The events of that morning on Main Street were shocking for the entire community which was not accustomed to this type of excitement. The news spread around town like a prairie fire. The locals made the robbery and shooting the subject of nearly everyone's conversation. As usual, some of the stories got exaggerated and twisted. On-lookers down on the street by the bank gawked at the small area cordoned off with yellow crime scene tape surrounding the old maroon Coupe de Ville. Police and sheriff's deputies continued their investigation well into the early evening.

Two days later a small private graveside service was held in the community cemetery on the east edge of town. Felicia, Chico, Sonya, Felicia's mother and Father Kiler from the Catholic Church were present. The priest offered a few consoling words and a prayer. The small group walked away as the two cemetery attendants lowered Robert's coffin into the ground. Felicia gave a huge sigh. Her mother noted an expression of total relief on her daughter's face. It was over at last!

In the years that followed Chico and Felicia enjoyed a very happy life together in their little house in Bender. Following Robert's death, Felicia was employed in the bank as a custodian. Each afternoon and on Saturdays after bank closing hours, Felicia could be found cleaning the bank's offices, board and meeting rooms and the large lobby. After six months, word spread around the bank that one of the tellers would be leaving soon.

John Chase, the 67 year old bank president had served in that capacity for nearly forty years and had brought it significant growth. He was admired by his employees and the townspeople. Mr. Chase could pass judgment on people well and he liked the work that Felicia had provided in keeping his bank clean. He knew what she and her son had been through. Calling her into his office one afternoon, he offered her the teller's job which was opening that week. Felicia was both surprised and gratified by his offer. She was trained and began her new position. In the years that followed it was a job she thoroughly loved.

Dr. Steve Harden had practiced medicine in town since completing medical school and Internship over twenty-five years ago. He brought his wife and a young family with him along with a heavy financial indebtedness acquired during the years of his education. The young doctor made a huge impression following his arrival in the community. Immediately he began serving the schools as a team physician. As a former athlete, he enjoyed working with the kids most of all.

During the past twenty-five years, Steve Harden developed a very busy medical practice. His two boys were outstanding athletes at Bender High School and subsequently graduated from college. His daughter also graduated from college after leaving Bender.

Chico also became an outstanding athlete for the Bender Broncos and excelled in the classroom with excellent grades. He has become fluent in Spanish, thanks to his mother's teaching at home. Since early childhood he always retained his special talent and interest in drawing.

In the beginning Chico and Dr. Harden had no special relationship with each other any more than the other athletes. That is, not until one cold blustery Friday night on the football field during his senior year. When he was a sophomore, the boy's size, speed and general football savvy had prompted the coaching staff's attention. They promoted him to the varsity from the JV team and since that time he has become an outstanding running back.

So on this particular night a significant event occurred for the young athlete and the physician which would eventually produce a very special bond between the two.

It was deep into the fourth quarter with one of Bender's arch rivals when Chico received the quarterback's hand-off and rolled around his right end. He was met with a crushing tackle by the defending outside linebacker. Chico was pummeled to the soggy cold turf. His left knee was twisted beneath the falling body of the opposing player. After trying to get up, Chico turned onto his side and grabbed his knee with severe pain. He continued to lay helpless on the field. The referee's whistle halted play while Dr. Steve Harden and two coaches ran onto the field and knelt down at Chico's side.

Later, it was found that Chico's injury did not require surgery but it did require several weeks of therapy which the office staff provided.

It was during this time of rehabilitation that a bond developed between the young man and his physician. Steve learned more about Chico's life and what the boy had accomplished with only his mother and absent father figure. On one of the many office visits during their usual conversation they learned of their mutual interest in art.

On the doctor's ranch a few miles outside town, a small rustic art studio sat near their ranch home. It was here where he could escape from the world of medicine whenever time permitted.

One fall day Steve invited Chico to spend the day out at the ranch with him. They spent a busy and enjoyable time together repairing fence, attending to the cattle and other things needing attention. Chico loved to be out there and enjoyed the doctor's companionship. After that day, Chico began working each weekend at the ranch side by side with a man he admired. For Steve, the presence of Chico beside him was like having another son.

In December Steve purchased a pair of high top leather cowboy boots and a pair of leather work gloves. Donna, the doctor's wife, wrapped the boots in a box with a large red ribbon. They attached a note that read: "Merry Christmas to Chico, the best damn ranch hand in Texas. From Doc and Donna." After receiving his gift, Chico said it was the nicest gift he had ever received in his life.

Felicia's bank salary was not sufficient to permit Chico's college entrance in the fall. The young man had given his future plans considerable thought. He elected to enlist in the Marines which would give him the opportunity for new experiences, new friends as well as the opportunity for travel. He planned to attend college after his stint in the military. Immediately following his high school graduation, Chico enlisted.

It was a tearful farewell when Felicia drove Chico to the DFW airport where he boarded a plane taking him to North Carolina for his basic training at Camp Lejeune. While driving home, Felicia couldn't help thinking how different life would be without her son around the house. She chuckled when recalling that Chico had never been farther from home than Fort Worth.

Throughout his basic training, Felicia could tell Chico was becoming a very proud Marine. She kept a colored photo of him in his uniform on the nightstand next to her bed. Every night before turning out her light, she would give a smart salute to her Marine.

Steve Harden had occasional phone conversations with Chico during his training at Lejeune. Chico always asked about things on the ranch and always commented how he missed the good times they shared out there.

With his intense training nearing completion, word came that Chico's unit was making immediate plans for embarkation to Baghdad, Iraq. It was nearly three weeks before Felicia received word that her son was finally there.

Today, one week later, Dr. Harden had been snowed under with office appointments. It was just one of those days with the office phones ringing constantly. One of the calls came from Steve's close friend, Bill Greenwell, the Postmaster. So as not to bother Steve, Bill gave a message to Margie, the office receptionist.

Margie grabbed a note pad and scribbled a note to Dr. Harden: "Mr. Greenwell said you have a package at the post office too large for delivery. He requests you pick it up at your convenience." She placed the note on Steve's desk.

By noon the office staff had cleared out the last of the morning's schedule permitting time for Steve to grab a bite of lunch. Steve picked up Margie's note along with his jacket and rushed out to his car. He reminded himself as he read her note to stop by the post office after lunch on his way back to the office.

Following a quick lunch, Bill and the doctor exchanged greetings and a brief exchange about last Sunday's Cowboy game up in Green Bay. Cutting the chat short, Steve picked up the package and hurried back to his office.

At his office Steve began to unwrap the package. It was over 24 inches in length and width and wrapped with several layers of heavy brown paper sealed with strips of wide tape. His address was labeled clearly, yet the return address was smudged either by water or perhaps grease.

Steve removed the layers of soiled paper with care and eventually removed a white piece of cardboard on which he found a brilliant detailed pencil drawing showing three Marines dressed in combat fatigues, armed with AK47 rifles, and standing in front of a military HumVee vehicle. In the lower right hand corner of the drawing appeared the artist's signature – Chico O'Neil. Inside the wrappings Steve found a note with the following inscription:

"Hi Dr. Harden: Well, I finally made it over here. I wanted to make you a sketch to remember me while I'm gone. How are the cows? Hope all is well with you and Mrs. Harden. Thanks for everything. Your friend, Chico"

Steve swallowed hard as he looked at the drawing and then reread his note. He was so damn proud of that young man.

Exactly one week after receiving Chico's drawing which was now framed and hanging in the office waiting room for all to see, Steve hurried out for his noon lunch at the Bender Café. Fred Glass, owner of the cafe, was behind the serving counter and after seeing Steve enter, began drawing him his usual glass of iced tea. Fred then asked, "Hey Doc, have ya heard the latest?"

Before Steve could respond to his question, Fred answered, "Bender has just had its first war casualty in Iraq – a 19 year old Marine. He was that great running back we had the last three years – Chico O'Neil."

About the Author

Stan Briney's penchant for creativity and detail is well-known in his art endeavors; however, it was only after he had successfully published his life story called "Self Portrait" that his interest was drawn to free-lance fiction writing. With this interest has now come this anthology of moving and action-packed stories.

At a very young age, while growing up in the Midwest, the author displayed a gift for drawing. He graduated from medical school after receiving both Bachelor and Master degrees at the State University of Iowa. With a specialty practice in Radiology he enjoyed a long distinguished career in medicine while living in Fort Worth, Texas.

While nurturing his interest in art throughout life, following his retirement in 1995, he has established a successful new career as a professional artist. Today his award-winning bronze sculptures, pencil, and pen/ink drawings are found in private collections, schools, homes, and offices throughout the United States and abroad.

Briney and his wife reside in their country home in the cattle ranching area of north central Texas where he has his studio and gallery.

Manufactured By: RR Donnelley
                     Breinigsville, PA USA
                     January, 2011